92565

F
Gor

Gorog, Judith

On meeting witches
at wells

14 95

DATE DUE			
MAR 14 '00	OCT 18 '00		
NOV 28 '96			
FEB 06 '97	MAR 07 '01		
46 5 1 '00	MAR 18 '01		
NOV 04 '97	DEC 19 2001		
SEP 24 '98	NOV 06 2002		
OCT 20 '98			
MAR 18 '99			
SEP 18 '99			
JAN 25 '00			
SEP 15 '00			

ON MEETING

WITCHES

AT WELLS

On Meeting Witches at Wells ❖

JUDITH GOROG

PHILOMEL BOOKS
New York

Philomel Books, a division of The Putnam & Grosset Book Group,
200 Madison Avenue, New York, New York 10016.
Published simultaneously in Canada.
The poem "Joy," from *An Unfinished Life* by Barbara Boggs Sigmund
Copyright © 1990 by Barbara Boggs Sigmund.
Reprinted by permission of The Arts Council, Princeton.
Book design by Sara Reynolds
The text was set in Baskerville No. 2

Library of Congress Cataloging-in-Publication Data

Gorog, Judith.
On meeting witches at wells / by Judith Gorog.
p. cm.
Summary: A collection of dark short stories told in a Scheherazade
fashion for middle readers.
ISBN 0-399-21803-3
1. Horror stories, American.   2. Children's stories, American.
[1. Horror stories.   2. Short stories.]   I. Title.
PZ7.G6730n   1991   90-20101 CIP AC
[Fic]-dc20

First impression

J O Y

Last week I found joy
On the living room floor.
It had fallen out of a drawer . . .

Joy was written on a gaily
            painted card,
And I picked it up and pinned
            it to the mantel
For a talisman, a magnet
To draw happiness
Down the chimney,
From above. . . .

Barbara Boggs Sigmund

CONTENTS

❖ Poor Farm Road School

L ike all old places, the school had all sorts of traditions. There was a pie feast in the fall, with vegetable
pies, meat pies, fruit, berry, chocolate, every possible kind
of luscious pie. The whole town came out to taste and
feast. There was a soap-bubble-making day in the spring,
as well as another day for the making and flying of kites
of every description. The oldest tradition was, however,
reserved for the eighth-graders. It seemed a harmless
way for the graduating class to spend time during the
last week of school. Three members of the staff had under-
taken the job for as long as anyone could remember:
Ms. Laurel, the eighth-grade teacher; Ms. Holly, the
school librarian; and Ms. Oakes, the school secretary.
Those three would assemble cloth, pins, needles, thread,
and a seemingly endless supply of old parachutes, which
had been made from rayon dyed a most astonishing array
of colors.

During the hot sleepy days of June, the week before
promotion, the eighth-grade students would sit out on the
grass under the trees. Each of them made a pillow while
one of the three adults told them stories. You could make

your pillow as elaborate or as simple as you chose. The pillows made a nice memento; lots of families in town had them. There were those who claimed that by putting your head upon one of those story pillows, you could hear . . . well, stories.

At four o'clock on a bleak November Thursday, the school building, which everyone in town habitually described as being solid as a rock, developed a large crack that ran from the top of the second floor, outside the fifth-grade classroom, right down to the top of the second-grade classroom beneath it.

On Friday, the school was closed. The engineer who examined the building was made uneasy, not so much by the crack, which seemed to have stabilized, but by the groaning and creaking she heard while making her inspection of the inside of the building. It was strange, for she could not measure any movement, though she certainly did hear it.

Just to be safe, movers were summoned to take away the furniture and books. They worked hard all day until dusk, muttering all the while that getting paid for overtime was nice, but the creaks and groans of the building were unsettling. Furthermore, after dark the movers could not check the size of the crack each time they delivered a load to the trucks parked outside the building.

On Friday, the children had a day off from school. On Friday night, the school board and the town council met to decide whether or not the building could be repaired. At dawn on Saturday morning, the movers returned to take away the last of the furniture and books. They regarded the crack warily. ♦

"WE THOUGHT we'd have forever," Ms. Oakes muttered for the third or fourth time. But now nobody knew how much time was left. If they were going to do the pillows at all this year, it had to be now. Jeff and Sidney sat in the school office shredding rayon into fluff. Part of the class was off somewhere in the building with Ms. Laurel, the rest in the library with Ms. Holly.

On the desk in front of Jeff, a rainbow pile grew. Absently, he swept it into a canvas bag. Sidney popped her bubble gum. Ms. Oakes looked up from the box of papers she was sorting. Sidney grimaced, then made a big show of chewing silently. The moving men clattered down the hallway, pushing dollies laden with desks. Jeff was about to say how sad it was, how he'd always imagined himself coming back to the old school to visit, when one of the ladies from the cafeteria appeared at the doorway. Ms. Oakes didn't seem surprised to see the lady. Jeff was. After all, the only thing left of the cafeteria was a dark room full of rust spots marking the places where the huge stoves and food lockers had stood on the floor. In the gloom you could see dark smudges outlining where cabinets had stood against the walls. Who would want to see that?

The lady was nice, although Jeff had always been shy

around her because of her gold tooth. He tried so hard not to stare at it, but felt unable to keep his eyes away.

"Hullo Jeff, Sidney," the cafeteria lady said, tooth glittering. "You're at work on the story pillows?"

"Yeah."

"I'll help you for a while. It would be a shame if you did pillows without my telling you about the Cub Scout and the raptor lady." But the cafeteria lady sat herself down on a chair someone had squeezed next to the copying machine, and started to shred purple rayon into a pile on her lap without saying a word. Sidney offered her a stick of gum, to which the cafeteria lady simply said, "No, thank you."

Jeff looked down at his own hands pulling at the soft cloth. Why didn't she say anything? It was too quiet. Jeff wished the moving men would come back with their carts.

"You were going to tell us about . . . ," Ms. Oakes encouraged.

"Ah, yes. Pip. That Pip. Now there was a boy. . . ."

❖ The Cub Scout and the Raptor Lady

Pip could run and shoot baskets and hike and jump and swim just like the other Cub Scouts. At the monthly pack meetings he could be restless in his chair just like the other Cub Scouts. In the circle he sometimes giggled, just like the others. For the most part, Pip got praised and scolded just as often as the others did.

There was, however, one thing that caused Pip all sorts of trouble: his imagination.

Now, the other scouts told tall tales; they exaggerated; they made wild claims. But when Pip got started, the rest of the kids stood aside goggle-eyed until some grown-up showed up to stop Pip's story. Trouble was, anything at all could set him off, even a tiny bump in the sidewalk. Pip talked so fast, and combined big words and small ones so unevenly, that half the time the kids who heard Pip only got half the story; and when they repeated the half they got, it was so wild but somehow so convincing, that even the grown-ups half believed. It took forever to straighten out anything anyone heard from Pip. To make matters worse, Pip was interested in everything from rocks to

5

microbes, and sometimes the wild stories he told were indeed true, or nearly true.

Pip left most grown-ups feeling exhausted. He seemed always to be on the wrong side of every teacher at school, of every scoutmaster. Only Mr. Toolie, one of the scout leaders, would gently redirect the conversation when Pip was being scolded for his "wild imagination." The other grown-ups kept saying to him, "Pip, you must learn to control your imagination!"

The Cub Scouts had weekly den meetings at seven-thirty on Monday nights, and pack meetings at seven o'clock on the third Wednesday of the month. All of the dens, from those with the youngest cubs to those with the biggest boys—the ones who would be Boy Scouts next year—went to the pack meetings.

Pack meetings were painfully long, so long that most of the boys felt the need to run outside and chase each other at least once during the evening. Nevertheless, no one wanted to miss a pack meeting. There was always something special about it. There were ceremonies. Often there were awards given, and a Cub Scout felt proud to be called up for an award. Best of all, there were amazing and wonderful programs at the pack meetings.

At one pack meeting, Pip had watched a famous chemist make explosions, some with color and light, some with satisfyingly loud noises. Two Cub Scouts had been chosen to help the chemist. One hundred other Cub Scouts watched, each wishing he had been chosen.

Those once-a-month pack meetings in the Poor Farm Road Elementary School cafeteria/auditorium were important. It was the last pack meeting of the spring when the raptor lady came. Pip was there early, helping to set up the folding chairs, when the tiny gray old lady limped into the auditorium. She carried one small covered cage.

Some of the Cub Scouts stared at her, shy. Two brave boys asked if they could help.

"No, thank you," the lady answered in a rasping whisper. "They are frightened now and need to be calmed. If you could keep the room as quiet as possible?"

Pip had already stopped scraping the chairs on the floor. He and the other boys moved as quietly as they could, looking often at the covered cage sitting up on the front of the stage. The old lady brought in more cages, one by one, both square and round, each of them covered with a dark cloth.

Watching her limp in and out of the auditorium, Pip wondered if walking hurt her. The heavy brown shoes looked so much like rocks covering her feet. Gray-and-brown tweed skirt, gray sweater, gray hair, fierce eyes behind her glasses, she looked like someone who could both frighten and love you. After she had brought in six cages, the lady sat down on a chair near them, sat very still and said nothing.

It seemed forever to all the Cub Scouts before the meeting had begun and the guest speaker was introduced.

Never had the boys been so still.

The lady began by telling them which birds were raptors. As she spoke the word "hawk," Pip's heart soared right out of his chest. How many times had he drawn a hawk, pinned it up in his room, dreamed that when he awoke the hawk had become real and flown away? How many times had he imagined the hawk had come back to be his friend forever?

The lady told how she had come to take care of injured raptors, where she did her work, and how she cared for them. Then, slowly, one by one, she uncovered the cages and told about the birds inside.

This young owl had been caught in a soccer net, this one in the string of a kite snarled in a tree. That hawk had been wounded by a gun. These two hawks had been stolen from their nest by someone who wanted them for pets. The raptor lady had received them half-starved because their captor did not know how to care for them.

Pip felt guilty for every soccer net, for every kite, for every piece of fishing line, for every hook that had hurt a bird. At the same time, he was longing to touch those birds. Every Cub Scout in the room asked to touch them, but the raptor lady said no. She told them about the good that raptors do in the wild, and why they must be wild. Pip listened and watched. How much like an owl the lady was, how soft her feathers, how piercing her eyes. Back and forth from lady to owl she changed as she talked to them, Pip watching all the while.

And then the talk was over.

8

To Pip's joy and amazement, the raptor lady walked right up to where he sat. She asked Pip, in her scratchy whisper, to help her carry the birds outside. This was no wild imagination! Pip had been chosen. While the other boys were called to the back of the auditorium to receive assignments for the next camping trip, Pip put covers on cages. He moved as slowly as the old lady herself. He could smell the hawk smell, the owl smell, feel and hear the birds as they rustled inside their cages.

One by one Pip and the raptor lady carried them outside. One by one they put the cages into the opened back end of a battered station wagon.

When the last cage had been set down, the old lady did not close the tailgate of the station wagon. No. She turned to Pip. "Go back." She pointed toward the auditorium door. Pip had hoped for one more minute near the raptors. "Go back and close the door," she repeated. "Then come help me." Pip did as she had ordered, running both ways.

The old lady had already begun taking the covers off the cages. "This," she said, "is a large open space, with fields and forest for miles on all sides; all of it protected . . . a perfect spot." Pip stared at her. Again, he could see her shifting, shimmering. Right there in front of him, the raptor lady was becoming all feathers, wings, beak, two bright eyes.

"Help me open the cages," the raptor lady insisted, becoming a human lady once again. "There isn't much time."

Pip gently opened the cage nearest to him.

"It's spring. Time to go," the raptor lady whispered. "Put your hand in. Let him stand on it. Then take him out and raise your hand; like this," she instructed.

Pip slowly put his fist into the cage. Without hesitation the young hawk grasped it with its claws. Slowly, feeling his own heart tearing at his chest, Pip raised his arm and held up his fist. The hawk seemed reluctant to leave.

"He'd prefer daylight," sighed the raptor lady, "but it has to be now, and the full moon will help some. Throw your fist into the air."

Pip did so, and saw the hawk soar, circle, and fly away. After that it was easier; the second hawk soared; and the third. Then one after the other, with the raptor lady encouraging him, he released the owls, who made soft cries as they went.

Turning back to the station wagon after the last of the owls had disappeared, Pip saw that the raptor lady no longer had those heavy brown rocks on her feet. She was settled there on the tailgate, all feathers, one good claw, one crippled. Pip stared. She was the biggest owl he'd ever seen. But how could she hunt with only one claw? Blinking at him in the moonlight, she fluttered her great wings. Pip could hear that rasping voice: "Pip. Don't worry. I can take care of myself, but, please, are you strong enough to throw me up, too?"

Pip nodded. He could.

Then standing on the back of the tailgate, Pip raised his

fist. The owl, grasping it with her one good claw, stretch-ed, reached, flapped, *flew*. Up, up in a rush of feathers and whirring wings. She circled once, gave that soft cry, and then straight into the light of the full moon she flew. The rush of air made Pip's eyes water. He climbed down, wondering what would happen to the station wagon.

Walking slowly back to the auditorium door, Pip was thinking about how he'd have to go around to the other entrance because that door always locked when it closed. But no, it was open just a crack, although he had closed it securely. Had someone been standing there?

Once inside, Pip started helping Mr. Toolie stack up the chairs. Mr. Munday came up to Pip, smiling and chuck-ling. Of all the scout leaders, he was the one Pip liked least. Munday was always doing embarrassing things, like stopping you to tell you in a loud voice in front of a lot of other people just how he thought you could improve your-self. Or else he'd tell you that you really could be a leader among boys if you would only change and be what he told you to be. He'd tell you how much he liked you, how he was your *friend*. Now Mr. Munday called all the boys who were stacking chairs. "Gather round, scouts! Pip, we were looking for you earlier. You get an award tonight. This is the first time at a pack meeting. . . ." He held out his hand for Pip to shake, and handed him a heavily embroidered circle of cloth with the other. "The Cub Scout self-control award to mark the first time you have *not* let your wild imagination run away with you. Congratulations!"

His face burning red, Pip shook hands, took the award, and mumbled, "Thank you."

Mr. Munday marched off, followed by most of the boys. Slowly the others drifted away.

Pip and Mr. Toolie continued stacking the chairs until they were all put away and the auditorium was empty. They were starting to turn out the lights, when Mr. Toolie laughed, which startled Pip.

Mr. Toolie stopped, his hand on the row of light switches. "She was so impatient, with spring and the full moon, impatient enough to up and fly right out of this room. I warned her that you'd see what none of the others could see." Mr. Toolie shook his head. "And think of all the trouble that would have caused you." He turned off the last of the lights. "You'd never have got your award." ♦

"DID THAT HAPPEN at this school?" Jeff asked, while Sidney stared, her gum stopped still in her jaw.

"That's the way I heard it, but then people do change stories in the telling," the cafeteria lady replied. "As I recall, there *was* a Pip, and he was quite a boy." She sighed. "I'll be going now. Good luck." The cafeteria lady pushed her pile of shredded rayon deep into the canvas bag beside Jeff's chair.

"Thanks," he said.

"Oh. Most welcome." The cafeteria lady waved good-bye as she opened the office door. The moving men had returned, and the racket in the hallway was terrific. Without looking back, the cafeteria lady closed the door and walked out of sight.

Slowly, Sidney started to chew once again, picking up speed as she shredded. One of the movers knocked on the glass window of the office, then beckoned to Ms. Oakes to come out and look at something in the hallway. Ms. Oakes left the office, shutting the door behind her.

The lights flickered, dimmed, grew bright.

"Oh, that again." Sidney snapped the gum in disgust.

"Yeah. And listen to the wind. Even in here I can hear it. It's as if I *feel* it." Jeff shivered.

Ms. Oakes returned, stumbling around the boxes that blocked the way to her chair. "The movers are leaving. Their van is full, and they say the building is groaning something fearful. I don't even hear it. Oh dear, when they come back they'll take the furniture in this room next and—how are you two doing?"

"Fine," Jeff said. "Look. Like they say, three bags full."

Ms. Oakes did not look, not even when Sidney popped her gum loudly. She was muttering over her desk drawers, all of which were stuck shut. "Well," she sat back with a sigh, "Whatever is in there does not want to come out, and so they can pack up the desk as it is. I'll find out later about those drawers. Here, give me some of that rayon. I need to calm my nerves. How are the others doing?"

"Kids are shredding pillow stuffing in the library. Ms. Holly is telling them stories, true stories, I think," Sidney managed to say around the gum. "And the rest are with Ms. Laurel somewhere. I dunno. Why do you need to calm your nerves?"

"Because . . . ," Ms. Oakes began, but stopped. Sidney and Jeff looked over at the chair next to the copying machine. The person sitting there was transparent, but getting stronger, a tiny old woman with a huge cardigan draped over her shoulders. "I know you don't have much time," she began. "Stories are flying. Heaven forbid this one should escape. You might miss hearing about Myra, who lived in that distant city."

❖ Myra

Myra was so lonely that she left messages on her own answering machine. At first it was just once in a while, but before long she called her apartment every day promptly at three-thirty in the afternoon.

"Hi, Myra," she'd say. "Just checking to see how you are." That was all she said at first, but then the messages got longer, hitting the important points. "Hi, Myra. Saw your new blouse this morning. Everyone admires how well you sew. You looked terrific! Feel like having chicken wings for dinner tonight? See you!" *Click*.

When Myra complained of her loneliness, as she often did, others would say, "Oh Myra, don't whine. Get out more. Forget yourself. Take up some interests!" But Myra did not want to forget herself. Thrifty Myra did not want to get out more. Myra knew exactly what kind of life she wanted. She wanted to be at home, all comfy, with someone who loved her. Myra knew, down to the finest detail, just how their life would be.

On one particular day, Myra was so miserably lonely that she almost missed seeing the ring. She was walking slowly, looking at her feet, when . . . well, maybe she felt the ring rather than saw it. Nevertheless, there it was. In the window of a tiny, dusty old jewelry shop it lay, a ring of dark gold, carved all around with fruits and flowers. It was the wedding ring for Myra, the only one for Myra in all the world. She had to buy it.

Without hesitating, Myra went into the shop, holding her breath while the jeweler took the ring from the window.

"Small," crooned the frail old goldsmith, "small for a delicate hand." Myra held out her hand for him to admire. She looked long at the ring, then at the old man.

"No," he said, as if she had asked him the question out loud. "It is the only one of its kind. I will not make another one like it. Never."

Myra had the strangest feeling that there was some story connected with the ring, but she did not want to know it, no indeed. That ring was for her, something real from her dream. Myra bought the ring, took it home, and slipped it on when she walked into her apartment.

From that day forward, she put the ring on when she got home, and took it off when she left. With that ring heavy on the third finger of her left hand, Myra could lead a married life at home. For a good, long while, Myra imagined and was happy.

Something like a year later, the imagining was not enough. Loneliness pulled at the edges of her mind, distracted her, pushed questions at her. Everyone else had someone. Why was she alone? Myra could not answer the question, but she did begin to examine her own imagined life. Did she *know* what she wanted? After some thought, she knew she did. Absolutely. The person to share it would be a man, a handsome man, as good-looking as — no, even better-looking than the ones her classmates or officemates had found. In the evenings Myra's husband would sit in his chair, she in hers, or sometimes on the sofa. He'd read. She'd knit or sew. Maybe he'd even read aloud to her. That would be fun. Occasionally they'd talk. He'd be interested in the things that happened to her at work. They'd listen to music.

Thinking hard, Myra found the answer. Of course! She needed his chair. She'd been picturing him in it all this time without realizing that she had never provided the very chair he had to have. Naturally, Myra went shopping for the chair, his chair, at her first opportunity. And Myra, knowing as she did exactly what she wanted, found it.

It was leather, very comfortable, and suited perfectly. The look and the leather smell of it gave her indescribable joy.

Then, for a very long time indeed, Myra came home from work, put on her wedding ring, and imagined while she made dinner. She imagined her husband sitting in his leather chair. How he'd enjoy her cooking! Of course, there would be times he'd insist that he cook, and while he did, she'd keep him company. Then, after dinner, Myra would sit knitting or sewing and imagine him sitting in his chair.

By this time, Myra knew exactly what her husband needed before he did, before the loneliness pulled and pushed at her. It was so clear; he needed a pipe, and an ash tray of course. Later, looking at her own furry slippers, she bought leather slippers for the man she imagined in the leather chair.

For months, Myra imagined her life with her husband and how comfortable it was, until the day Myra got a bit of a surprise. The leather chair had been facing the window, looking out at the sunset of a Saturday afternoon. Myra sat on the couch, admiring the same view. Slowly the chair turned around, away from the window, toward Myra. The man in the chair was wearing the leather slippers Myra had bought for her imagined husband. He was lighting the pipe Myra had bought for her imagined husband. The slippers fit perfectly, and the man appeared to be quite at home; but *it would not do.*

"*NO!!!*" Myra started, and jumped up crying, "No! You're the wrong one! You're not young and handsome! You are an old man!" Myra cried big, hot tears. "You cannot look like that. I never, ever imagined you like that! No!" She was overcome with sobs.

Removing the pipe from his mouth, the man replied with the merest touch of gentle reproach in his voice. "Myra, dear Myra. With your wiry red hair standing out from your head like the top of a pineapple, and the thick soft down—although you bleach it regularly—upon your upper lip, do you really think you should make the demands you do?"

Myra did not give in. "No. I can only dream of young and

handsome. No!" With that, with all the anger and force she could muster, Myra imagined the too-old man away.

Life from then on was something of a struggle. Myra imagined her life as she would have it, worked her days in her office, and managed to keep the too-old man out of her sight. There were times, many times, she felt he was there, but Myra refused to see him.

Years passed, until one day Myra became sick with the flu. Taking advantage of her weakness, the too-old man appeared once more in the chair. "Poor baby," he said. "Shall I bring you some broth?"

"You don't look quite so bad to me now. How can that be?" Myra groaned out of her flu misery.

"You look fine to me, sick or well," chuckled the too-old man fondly. "Broth?" he offered once again.

Myra shook her aching head. "I won't give in so easily. I still think you are too old." Groggy with the flu, Myra stared at the man, trying to see him clearly. After a moment, she gave up and went to sleep.

Once she was well, however, Myra spent a great deal of time thinking about the man who had twice forced himself into her imagined life. And the more she thought, the better she felt, because he had looked exactly the same the second time she saw him as he had the first. It wasn't so much that he was younger or better-looking, but that he had not gotten worse with time. Stubborn, stubborn Myra, pleased as she was, continued to keep the man out of her imagined life.

She let a few more years pass, accumulated a few more wrinkles of her own, and then one afternoon skipped her telephone call to her answering machine. Leaving the office that day, Myra slipped the wedding ring onto the third finger of her left hand and imagined all the way home. Sure enough, when she closed the apartment door behind her and walked into the living room, the leather chair, wreathed in aromatic pipe smoke, turned from the window.

"Hullo. I have decided that I love you," Myra said, leaning over to kiss the not-so-very-old man.

"I love you, too," he replied.♦

HER MOUTH SET in a tiny smile, the old lady bowed to them and then faded from sight. After a time, Ms. Oakes sighed.

"Are you still nervous?" Sidney asked.

"Less, but, that is—I should *not* complain. Instead, I *should* tell you how glad I am that you are here to help with the pillows. What made you come? And didn't your parents stop you? After all, that crack certainly has the movers feeling uncomfortable in here."

"My mom was trying on wigs." Sidney shifted her wad of gum. "I waited until she was in a frenzy of indecision, and told her, 'Bye, I'm going to school.' She never noticed."

"Wigs?" Ms. Oakes peered over the top of her glasses.

"She's got, I dunno, maybe thirty, all colors; straight, curly. They never struck you?"

"I guess not."

"I said I was going to do a job for Ms. Laurel," Jeff interjected. "They were deep in the morning paper."

"I see," Ms. Oakes said. "But, then, why *did* you come?"

Sidney and Jeff both shrugged. "Had to . . . a feeling."

"Mmm. I was hoping, but I did not summon. No. No. No. I did not. It didn't seem fair." She rushed so that her words were all run together. "Neither did Ms. Holly nor Ms. Laurel summon; I know because I asked them. We must give a pillow to every child from this school, don't you see? The little ones won't be here for nine years the way you have been. You have nine years of magic to protect you. They need the pillows." She took off her glasses and pretended to polish them.

"Ahh . . . Ms. Oakes?" Sidney shifted uneasily in her chair. "If you talk about all this sad stuff, instead of telling stories, will it go into the pillows, too? Will stories go in that we can't hear?"

"Yes, to both questions," said Ms. Oakes. "So, I'd best get cracking." She cleared her throat. "As you both know, hearing stories while the kids sat working was one of the traditions that went along with making the pillows. . . ."

"Yeah," interjected Sidney, "under the trees outside, the whole last week of school . . . June, hot sun, shade, lemonade . . . Not exactly what we have here: November with the building falling down. What a gyp!"

"Sorry about that. But you have it exactly. It was a tradition of more than a hundred years. Every graduating class made them, since the school began. In the olden days, when the school first opened, most children didn't go past the eighth grade. Into the pillows went bits of history, stories—real and unreal—tales, and fragments. It was something good for them to take away."

"Still is," said Jeff. "My dad has his, and my grandfather's."

"The building's not gonna be fixed?" Sidney asked. "Why not?"

"Everyone in town thinks it will be, but we—Ms. Holly, Ms. Laurel, and I—know otherwise. The well wants it back."

"The well?"

She took off her glasses and put them on her desk. "More than two hundred years ago, a county 'poor farm' was built on this spot. It was a place where people could go who had lost their own farms, or their houses in the village, because of debt. In general, it was the place where widows and orphans could find shelter for short or long periods when they could not work their farms alone, or when death or illness or desertion left them with no means to manage. It was a working farm, grew its own food, and if anything was left after feeding the people living here, it was sold and the profits were used to pay off the debts of any residents. It sounds gloomy, and many poor farms or almshouses around the world were awful places, but this one was not sad at all.

"About a hundred years ago, the poor farm was no longer needed. The buildings were pulled down. This school was built on the same spot, using some of the same bricks and timber. Some of the former orphans had since grown up and become successful in farming, business, or as artisans. They wanted to do something for the school. One family gave the oaken bannisters, another the ironwork on the staircases. Everyone got involved in a huge debate about naming the school. Some people argued that Poor Farm Road Elementary School sounded sad to the newcomers who were moving to the county, and said we needed a name more *uplifting*. The opposing view was that we should know our history and that the poor farm was part of it, and even a good part of it. As you know, the latter view won. So for over one hundred years, a school has stood on this spot."

"Until the wall cracked," Sidney said.

"Yes. Until the wall cracked."

"You said the poor farm was never sad. Never?"

"It was a place . . ." She sighed. "Sorry. It makes me sad now to think about it. But never mind." Drying her eyes, she rushed on. "The poor farm had a well with wonderful sweet water, a well that never went dry in any drought. That well had as its source an ancient spring, a spring that had spirits more powerful than most people could ever imagine. How or why the spirits of the spring allowed the poor farm to be built over it, and then the school afterward, covering the spring for more than two hundred years, well, my dears, we don't understand it at all, but that is what happened. Lots of people knew about the well. It was in history books. But most people assumed it had gone dry. Truth is, the spring simply went deep into the earth, but it has come back and is taking back its place, and right now."

"You mean," Jeff paused with a handful of fluff over the canvas bag, "this school will go underwater, a lake?"

"Wonderful." Sidney stopped chewing. "Now?"

"Certainly very soon."

"Weird. How do you know?"

"After we saw the crack in the wall, we asked."

"You asked the spring?"

"Mmm. Yes. Now I'll take these filled bags up to Ms. Laurel to mix with the rest of the stuffing. I want to see how the others are. Be right back.

"Oh, there may be more visitors. That old lady was principal here long, long ago. Others will come, too, because everything is all stirred up, the past, near, far, things whirling around."

"Kinda like an electrical storm, wild radio signals, whirlpools, stuff like that." Jeff wanted to reassure Ms. Oakes, who was pretty weepy. He looked at the clock, then at his watch. "Humph."

"What's up?" Sidney resumed popping her gum as soon as Ms. Oakes closed the office door.

"Time in here today is like a rubber band. Look, the

clocks, and my watch, too, they run for three minutes, then stop for a while. There is no way we have been here only an hour."

"Naw. My gum has lost its flavor twice. If I add any more, my jaw will break."

The two little girls who came into the office did not appear to notice the loud snap of Sidney's gum. They held hands and whispered to one another. Jeff stared at them, wanting to touch them. The cafeteria lady had looked real, the old lady definitely whispy. These girls seemed like a couple of regular little kids, a kindergartner and maybe a second-grader. With big eyes, they whispered to one another as if they were timid, all alone in a big place.

Sidney looked hard at Jeff, then whispered, "They make me feel as if *we* are invisible spirits."

Jeff motioned for Sidney to listen. What was that? What were the girls saying?

❖ Remember?

Remember the house around the corner? Remember the family that lived there? The father was a student at the divinity school, and worked as a carpenter. The mother was a nurse. The big boy was always nice to little kids. When he and the other big boys and girls played ball in the alley, he always let us play, too. The boy had an elder sister, who was a ballerina. The mother sewed for the big sister and for several others at the ballet society, costumes that looked like dreams. That big sister was so beautiful we didn't even dare to say hello to her.

We never ever saw those kids on Halloween. We only dared to go to their house because both Daddy and Mommy came with us. It took every bit of our courage to go there at all, but we never missed. We waited until dark. Then, holding tight to our parents' hands, we approached the stone steps of the house around the corner.

Up the steps we went, swallowing hard. On Halloween night, the porch door always stood ajar. Before we could ring the bell, the inner door silently swung open. We could hear tinkly piano music that broke off in the middle of a phrase. During the long silence that followed, you could hear your own heart pounding in your ears. Then, *plinkity plunk,* the music began again.

We never said "trick or treat" at the house around the corner. As we slowly approached the opened door, a soft voice called to us. "Ahhhhhh, visitors. Dooooo commmmme innnnnnn." A pale hand motioned from inside.

Trembling, we stepped over the threshold.

Cobwebs trailed from the ceiling, from draperies, walls and light fixtures, all swaying gently. A pale woman in a long dress of tattered lace stood shimmering in the center of the room. She seemed to float there, waiting. Candles sputtered. The woman stepped to one side, motioning us to take something from the table that had been hidden by her skirts.

We gasped.

The low round table was covered with a pale pink cloth. On it rested a huge silver-colored platter. On the platter was a bed of curly parsley. On the parsley was the bearded head of a man, our neighbor.

"Have a grape, dear," the woman cooed to the head.

The man's mouth opened wide. In went the grape, fed to him by the woman's pale fingers.

Crunch. Crunch. The grape had seeds. The man's head smiled at us. He winked.

We trembled.

Time to go. Daddy and Mommy pried us from our spot. They said good night. We could not manage to make a sound.

At the foot of the steps were more children wearing their costumes, holding their treat bags, hesitating before they started up to the door. They stared at us. Did they know what was waiting inside? Did they dare to go?

We were halfway around the corner, on the way home, before we could begin to giggle, to ask each other, "Did you see? Did you see?"

Every year there was a different scene in the house around the corner. Every year there was different music. We talked about that house all year long, warned scaredy kids that they should stay away. And if we saw the bearded carpenter-minister neighbor in the daytime and mentioned Halloween, he always replied, "Oh, Halloween? You were out trick-or-treating? I'm sorry if we missed you. I guess nobody was at home at our house."

Remember the house around the corner? I'll go there with you this Halloween—if you'll hold my hand. ♦

THOSE LAST WORDS were whispered by the smaller of the two girls as she turned, held out her hand, and looked directly at Jeff.

"Yeah. Sure. I'll come." Jeff half stood, reaching for her outstretched hand. The little girl smiled, appeared to blush at Jeff's stare, then looked back at the older girl.

"Bye." That was Sidney whispering. "Didn't you hear her?" she asked Jeff. "She said bye to me."

They were both grinning after the children, as if they were some terrific find that they wanted to take home. The girls, however, did not look back after they had turned away, but went straight to the office door. They opened the door, then paused in the doorway, where they stroked and petted an enormous black dog. After wagging her tail at the girls in greeting, and accepting a kiss from each of them on the top of her head, the animal came into the room and sat down. Then with great dignity, the dog turned her golden-brown eyes first to Sidney, then to Jeff. "Good morning. How is your work coming along?"

"Oh, pretty good," Jeff replied.

"How about you?" Sidney asked politely.

The dog gave a great sigh. "I was born in this place, in a supply closet down the hall, and have since ranged the world over. I have returned now and then. . . . My story for you is one of a poor dog, a *sweet* dog. Believe me! It begins with a man shouting . . .

❖ Juno

"**H**ey! Lady! Is that your dog? Well, hold on to her. I don't like the way she's looking at me."

Oh dear, oh dear, thought Ms. Dunne. *I wonder myself.*

Ms. Dunne held Juno on a short leash until the man was safely out of sight. Then, with a sigh of resignation, Ms. Dunne turned homeward. Poor old Juno, disappointed, lagged behind. How could the walk in the park possibly be that short? Juno grinned, wagged her stub of a tail, and licked at Ms. Dunne's hand. Ms. Dunne pulled her hand away. Poor Juno. Nothing helped. They went home. Ms. Dunne reproached herself. That man didn't know. He couldn't know. And besides . . .

Ms. Dunne put the leash away in its place. She was a tidy woman, in a tidy little house. Anyone could find the kitchen linen drawer in her house, or a cup and saucer, she was that orderly. Anyone could easily find anything in Ms. Dunne's house, with its order so easily perceived.

Large, cheerful Juno had been a joy to Ms. Dunne. Juno was herself a tidy, well-mannered, short-haired dog, who had easily been taught to stay off the furniture, and always to walk politely on the leash. True, Juno had once, quite unintentionally, frightened the mailman. Her bark was loud and sharp, and the mailman's big bag had excited her. Seeing him for the first time, she had barked and barked at him, demanding to be let out the screen door to explore that wonderful bag. But Juno had even learned not to bark at the mailman. Now things had changed and the man in the park wasn't the only one afraid of Juno. Everyone had become afraid since that day. Sometimes Ms. Dunne even worried about herself.

She and Juno had led a quiet, tidy, ordered, affectionate existence for five years. That day, while Ms. Dunne was out visiting a friend, Juno had been locked inside the house as she always was. After a visit of about an hour, Ms. Dunne returned home to find Juno up on the couch!

This breach of trust would normally have called for severe discipline by Ms. Dunne, but poor Juno seemed to be sick as well. Juno coughed and gagged, and poor Ms. Dunne fretted for a minute before she got the leash and clicked it onto Juno's collar. Ms. Dunne didn't even notice the fresh spot on the floor by the closet door. Patting Juno affectionately on her poor sick head, Ms. Dunne led the dog out of the house, locked the front door, and got them both into the car. Off they drove to the vet, who examined Juno carefully.

"Yes, indeed," he murmured. "She's gagging on something."

"Ohhh." Ms. Dunne sighed in sympathy.

"Did she get into the garbage or something?" asked the vet, shaking his head.

"My Juno in garbage!" exclaimed Ms. Dunne. "Never!"

"Sorry," said the vet. "We'll soon find out what it is. We'll have to anesthetize her. That will take time. No need to wait here, Ms. Dunne. I'll telephone you. Don't worry."

But Ms. Dunne did worry all the way home. As she got out of her car, she could hear, through the kitchen window, the sound of her telephone ringing. She ran the few steps across the drive and up the stairs, then unlocked the back door. Once inside, she grabbed the telephone in midring. It was the vet.

"Please leave your house. Go to your neighbor's, and telephone me from there."

Baffled, Ms. Dunne nodded. *Click.* The vet had hung up his telephone.

Ms. Dunne left her kitchen and went next door. Feeling very foolish, she rang the bell and asked if she could use the telephone. Of course she could.

By the time she finished dialing the number of the vet's office, Ms. Dunne could see one police car in front of her own tidy house, and another pulling into her drive, right behind her own car. The neighbor's children dashed to the windows. Five police officers ran to her house — front door, back door, looking at windows, checking the roof.

"Ms. Dunne?" The vet answered his telephone.

"Look! Look!" yelled the neighbor's children. "The police are taking a man out of Ms. Dunne's house!"

Ms. Dunne looked out the window. A man, carried between two policemen, wobbled out of her house. His right hand was wrapped in her second-best wool scarf, which had been hanging in its proper place next to her dark blue wool jacket in the front hall closet. A third policeman walked behind them, putting what looked like a large bag into a still larger clear plastic bag.

"Ohhh! Evidence!" yelled the neighbor's knowledgeable children.

"Ms. Dunne," repeated the vet. "What I found caught in Juno's throat was a human forefinger. It wasn't yours, so I called the police. Did Juno bite a burglar breaking into your house? Was he hiding from her? Was I right? Did the police find anything? Ms. Dunne, are you there?"

"Yes," Ms. Dunne had said that day. "I'm fine."

But of course she isn't fine, not fine at all. Ever since that day, Ms. Dunne cannot bear to see poor Juno lick her chops.♦

"POOR JUNO," Jeff said. "Now everybody thinks she's vicious?"

The black dog nodded her head sadly. "Worse. The word 'killer' has been used."

The dog and Jeff both jumped when Sidney's gum exploded loudly in what Sidney had imagined was a sympathetic pop.

"Well, children, I must go. Please keep Juno and her

story, and feel compassion for her." With that, the black dog arose and walked out of the office, closing the door behind her.

Jeff and Sidney sighed and stretched. Sidney looked long and hard at the wad of gum in her hand, then reluctantly put it into the wastepaper basket. "I may need to go home for more; not sure I can stay the rest of the time without it."

"I wonder where Ms. Oakes is," Jeff said.

"Yeah. We're nearly out of rayon."

"Let's finish what's here and go look for the rest of the class. All the fluff has to be mixed together anyway before we sew the pillows, mixed so that every pillow will get all the stories—right?"

"Yeah. Poor Ms. Oakes. She's gonna miss this school. Do you think she is some kind of witch? A nice one?"

"*Some* kind, and nice," Jeff agreed, turning as he spoke to see who was coming into the room from the darkened principal's office.

It was the tiny old lady in the large cardigan. She cleared her throat twice before she said, "I noticed that you two . . ." Her eyes glittered as she paused to stare first at Jeff and then at Sidney, who nodded their assent, not wanting to stop her in the telling. "You two were wondering about that golden wedding ring Myra bought. I could see that you were thinking there was something, something about that ring. Well sir, there was."

❖ Gypsy Gold

No one in the neighborhood could remember a time when the goldsmith had been a young man. Everyone alive knew his shop, knew the look of his straight, thick silver hair as he bent over his work. Everyone had watched those sinewy hands bring out from his display cases a watch, a necklace, a ring, a pair of earrings. A gift of gold to celebrate births, weddings, the religious ceremonies of growing up—that was a tradition for everyone in the neighborhood. All of them knew what the goldsmith made for them to give. As you walked past his shop or paused to look into the window, you unconsciously reached to touch the necklace or pin you wore, the cuff links at your wrists, the treasure he had made, something with memories.

No one alive in the neighborhood remembered that the goldsmith had once had a wife, and that she had died, and that he had lived for a long time alone in the apartment above his shop. No one remembered the goldsmith's youth or his first wife, but they all remembered the girl.

The girl was a gypsy of surpassing beauty. The neighborhood had awakened one morning to find a band of gypsies camped in a vacant store. You could tell the neighborhood was changing. It was the first time anyone knew of a vacant store in those parts. The gypsies had soaped over the front window, so no one knew how they lived inside. Except. They seemed to have no bedtime, no time when all was completely quiet.

The girl had appeared in the goldsmith's shop one summer day. To his surprise, she came in from the walled garden behind the shop. All at once he looked up from his work, and there she was in the open doorway, with the garden green behind her, the red of the geraniums to her right and left, the sun-gold dust motes dancing around her. The jeweler, who was no longer a young man, stared.

The girl held out her hand, palm up. There in the center of her palm was a piece of quartz. From where he sat, the goldsmith could see that it contained at least two nuggets of gold, each about the size of a pea.

"Goldsmith," sang the girl, "they say you make beautiful things. Make for me from this gypsy gold a ring to hold my love." She came across to the workbench in movements that made the goldsmith think of water, quick and gentle. He knew he could watch this girl forever.

"The ring I want," the girl whispered, "must have fruit and flowers all around, and be this wide." She showed him her finger. "Is there enough gold here for the ring?"

"Of course," replied the goldsmith, taking up his pencil. "Here," he began to sketch on a piece of brown paper. "Is this the ring you imagine?"

He looked up into the girl's face, and saw the surprise

and delight shining there. "Of course! You know exactly!" She touched the piece of quartz with her finger. "Is there enough gold here to make the ring and to pay you for your work?"

"Certainly," replied the goldsmith, while one voice within him was saying, "Loving her will break your heart," and another voice was replying sadly, "It already has."

And so the goldsmith set to work and made for the girl a ring to hold her love, but into that ring the goldsmith added gold of his own. Throughout the drawing, the making of the mold, the heating, pouring, cooling, finishing, the goldsmith worked. And while he worked, he hoped and wished with all his heart.

After he had completed the ring, he fashioned gold earrings. Into all three pieces he had put gypsy gold and his own, and all of his love unto the very last drop. Through the power of his artistry, his love, and the magic contained in the gypsy gold itself, he made beautiful things to capture and hold her, though his heart told him she had asked to have the ring made so that she could bind another to herself in lifelong love. It was wrong to bind her against her will; the jeweler knew it was wrong, and a dangerous thing to do, but he dared and hoped, and promised himself that he would make the girl so happy that she'd forgive him his trickery.

Then the goldsmith waited, dreaming and praying his love would truly be the stronger.

After some days, the girl appeared as she had before, from the garden. "We leave tomorrow," she said anxiously. "Is the ring made?"

The goldsmith nodded. The girl came over to the workbench. From the drawer behind him, the goldsmith took out two small, worn velvet bags.

"There was," he said, "so much gold in the quartz that I was able to make more than just your ring." Drawing out the earrings, he held them up for the girl to see.

"Ahh." She caught her breath. She found them beautiful, as he had hoped she would.

"Here. I made them for you," he urged.

Looking at him closely, as if she suspected a trick, the girl reached for the earrings, held them, admired them. Turning, she sought a looking glass, went over to it, and put the earrings into her ears. She smiled, tossed her hair. The goldsmith sighed.

Taking up the second velvet bag, the goldsmith said, "And now for the ring."

The girl returned to the workbench, leaned over and kissed the old man on the cheek. "Thank you," she said. "And was there really enough to pay you for your work?"

Instead of answering, the goldsmith took the ring from the bag. Taking the girl's hand, he slipped the ring onto her finger. Startled, she pulled back, but then stopped and looked at the ring.

"Its design is what I wanted," she said. "But I know what you have done." The look she gave the goldsmith was full of pity and sadness, and love. "Yes, I'll stay with you," she sighed. "Your love is very strong. But . . ." She came back, close to him, and stroked his cheek with her hand. "But, I cannot say how long this ring, which you have made your ring and not mine, can hold me here, and I feel sad to break your heart." The goldsmith held her hand to his cheek for a moment, then took it gently and kissed it.

The gypsies left. The girl stayed, became the goldsmith's wife. The garden flourished under her care, and with it the apartment and shop as well. The jeweler's rooms and garden had always been filled with pleasant light and shadow, for the goldsmith was an artist through and through. In the time of the young wife, however, the presence of beauty was so strong that passersby would stop, as if noticing for the first time all manner of things about the shop, the street, the garden glimpsed through the open doors.

"Would you look at that," someone would stop on the street and exclaim to himself. "Just see how the light strikes the window with its black frame, and that buttercup daring to bloom in the crack of the sidewalk just below it. The whole looks right, just so with the light like this. A fine sight, a fine day." With a sigh, the passerby would continue on his way.

Years later, when he looked back on it, the old man knew how powerful his love had been. He'd been happy and sad the whole time. So happy to have her there, but thinking always that today might be the first day of her leaving. He tried to keep her, tried with golden chains. He made works of the jeweler's art for her, inspired pieces. She was always pleased, and yet she always knew. The pieces were imbued with his love, and with them he hoped to hold her. Perhaps he had one of those secret half-formed thoughts that one should never have, the thought that she was greedy and that the gold itself would matter.

Summer and fall passed. At first, the winter went badly. Icy rains fell on the days when there was no icy wind to tear at skin and clothing. The young wife grew pale and silent. Then, when it seemed she could bear the winter no longer, the sun appeared, brilliant in the sky above the city. The goldsmith took up their coats, mittens, caps, and scarves, and helped the young wife put them on. He closed the shop and took her to a pond in the park. There they skated for as long as there was sun in the sky. After that, they skated when there was sun or wind or cold or snow. They skated every pond or stretch of river the city offered. Spring returned, but not the gypsies.

"Another gift?" she asked him when he gave her yet another golden bracelet. "But if I wear them all I will be unable to raise my hand to eat or drink." She laughed gently.

After that, the goldsmith gave her lilacs to plant in the garden. He stopped making rings and chains to hold her. He knew the time was surely coming. And so the summer passed, until one day the young wife was gone. She left behind all the rings and chains and bracelets. She left behind the ring she had asked him to make. She took only the earrings he had made for her from her gold and his and from his love. The note she left said only that he should not destroy the ring, but sell it someday to the person who would need it. "You'll know the one," the note had said.

No one in the neighborhood remembers a time when the old goldsmith was a young man. Everyone in the neighborhood remembers the girl who had been the goldsmith's young wife, and everyone in the neighborhood remembers the ring. Not one of them would buy a ring burdened with so much pain of love. Only strangers tempted fate by looking at the ring, and when the right one came along, the old man knew. ♦

"POOR OLD GUY."

"But Jeff, what if when she left him—" Sidney's words got all tangled in her rush to tell him. "What if after he put the ring on her finger and married her—what if when she left she didn't know it and he never knew it, but she had twins, a girl and a boy, and they came back because they wanted to know their father, and they loved the old jeweler and he got to be happy with them?"

"Yeah?" Jeff wasn't sure. He needed more time to think about it. He took the last piece of rayon, an orange-yellow one, and started shredding.

"I keep thinking." Sidney pushed a pile of fluff into an overflowing canvas bag.

"What do you suppose will happen to this building?" Jeff asked her.

"I think the spring is bubbling up under us; that it is gonna float this building right into the middle of a lake, like a huge old castle. Kids will swim out to it in the middle of the lake, and sunbathe on the gray stones, and hear the music you sometimes hear, and . . ."

Jeff shook his head. "I think there's gonna be a huge, I mean *huge*, crash, and the school building is gonna sink into a crack in the earth, with the spring way down at the pitch-black bottom of it. Icy water will flow around and above the school until there will be a huge lake, all blue-green water, clear as anything. And when you swim out into the middle of the lake, you'll see the building under you in the water, and dive down and swim around the building and through the openings that were windows. You'll be able to see inside, and there will be mysterious pictures and music you'll hear underwater. . . . Done! Last piece of rayon. You done, too?"

"Yup. Oh. The old lady is gone. I didn't even notice."

"Me neither. Maybe she'll come back. Thanks, lady," he called into the dark of the principal's office. "Hope you come to tell us some more. Hey Sid, let's lug this stuff upstairs to the classroom; see what the other kids are doing. We have to mix this stuff anyway. I wonder if, when ours is put together with what the others have done, we'll have enough to stuff all the pillows."

"Yeah. And what about sewing? That's gonna take time, too. Suppose any of the other kids have started the sewing?"

Struggling with the awkward canvas bags, Sidney and Jeff left the office and walked down the dim corridor, up the staircase, and toward the classroom. All the rooms were dark, empty, echoing their footsteps as they passed. Here and there pieces of tape fluttered on a bulletin board outside a classroom. Through the classroom doorways, they could see out the windows to the playground, where the wind tore at the trees and rushed at the edges of the stone building with a whine.

When they got to Ms. Laurel's classroom, Jeff set down his bags and reached for the door, which opened toward him slowly as he put out his hand for the knob. Jeff stepped back, stumbling over the bags at his feet. Sidney sneezed at the whiff of pipe smoke that came through the doorway.

"Sorry. Heard you coming and thought I'd help with the door." A small brown old man, bowlegged in leather chaps, smoking a beat-up black pipe, wearing a real cowboy hat on his head and leather gloves on his hands, stood in the doorway. Behind him the rest of the eighth-grade class sat in a ragged circle on the floor, with a mountain of shredded rayon fluff in the approximate middle of the group.

"We were gonna come look for you," Eustace said. "Have you seen Ms. Laurel?"

"No. Not her, not Ms. Oakes, not Ms. Holly. Where are they?"

"Dunno."

"Oh, don't worry about them." The old cowboy spoke up. "They're fetching the cloth you'll need for the pillow covers. I'll just set with you a spell, if you don't mind, before I get on my way."

"Where are you going?" Eustace asked.

"Did you go to this school?"

"Me? No. I courted a girl from here, though, long time ago. I been just about everywhere, and keep on going, checkin' on people the way I used to check on cattle."

He poked in his pipe, puffed, and sat down on the edge of Ms. Laurel's desk. "I figured you'd wanna hear about something with a bit of evil in it, and luck and such."

His suggestion was met with general agreement, so he settled himself a bit further onto the top of the desk, and began. . . .

❖ The Thorn Branch

You can hear it whispered over half the county. "Brady leads a charmed life." Of course, no story is over till it's finished, but Brady's been closer to death than the whiskers of a nine-lives cat with one to spare.

One time, the first one I know about, happened when Brady was fourteen. Brady and his friend Mike had gone for a ride. They'd gone not too far, not too fast, just a ride before suppertime one spring evening on Mike's new motor scooter. Now, in those days no one had even heard of crash helmets, so the cool breeze blew the hair in and out of their eyes as the two boys rode along Seven Locks Road.

The car that swerved—"just to scare them," so the driver later claimed—was doing better than fifty the first time. That car, an old Chevy, had in it a pair of bullies. Neither of them had a license nor sense, and when the car swerved, Mike saw it and felt the rush of air and heard the tires. That car swerving so near to the scooter did make Mike tighten his grip on the handlegrips, and did make Brady tighten his hold on Mike's waist, but the boys continued on their way, not too fast, not too slow, a little ride before dinner. The old Chevy disappeared over the hill.

When the Chevy came back, "just to scare them," it was doing more than seventy; and when it swerved, it swerved too far and caught the scooter and sent it flying, and Mike and Brady went flying, too.

The bullies drove away fast, but then got worried and came back to see.

The scooter had been knocked pretty deep into the woods. Mike and Brady had bounced maybe once or twice, then slid a good way, stopping on their faces at the spot where the gravel turned to dirt alongside the road.

Minutes later, the Chevy pulled to a stop; the bullies looked around. Not a soul in sight. Those two cowards got out of the car, kinda tiptoed up to the still bodies of Mike and Brady. One look, and they agreed: The boys were dead. And it wasn't but a second later that the bullies decided it was best if no one knew what had happened.

One dragged Brady into the woods; the other dragged Mike. Quickly, they started to cover the boys with dirt. In harsh whispers they urged one another to hurry. The thing that bothered them most was how much they hated to bury the scooter. Oh, how they longed to take it out for a ride! Reluctantly, one bully went to work on burying the scooter.

Let me tell you that Brady is a lucky man, 'cause only his one hand was sticking ever so slightly out of that earth when a stablehand came out of that forest shortcut right close to where Brady lay. That fellow, he was hurrying along, headed home for his supper, an old man who worked for

Mike's father. That old stablehand surely did recognize that scooter, more or less covered with dirt and leaves. He surely did see that bit of Brady's hand sticking out of that pile of earth. And that stablehand knew just what to do. He ignored the bullies, who ran for the Chevy. He scraped away the dirt from Brady's face. He ran over to where Mike lay, under some low bushes at the edge of the forest. Then that old stablehand, he ran back through the shortcut to the barn for help. Saved those boys' lives, he did. As it was, Brady and Mike spent a good, long time in the hospital, not quite as long as the bullies spent in jail, but almost.

Years later, when Brady was a grown man, people still said, "Oh, Brady? Him that was buried alive? Sure. That's the one, a lucky man in fact."

Brady the grown man went into construction, built things all over the place. He was an on-site man, knew all about building from doing with his own hands and using his own mind. He was the kind to have his office in the other half of a storage shed, or in one corner of an equipment trailer, wherever.

Another thing about Brady. He had an eye, Brady did, and was forever finding things. That's how he got the thorn branch; just found it in some old woods. It was unusual, a broken piece on the ground, and the shape of it was like a sculpture, or something an artist would draw. Though Brady didn't talk much like that, about art 'n' such, he thought, and he noticed, and truly that silvery branch, all covered with thorns, was beautiful. So he carried it back to the office and set it on the windowsill.

It was the thorniest branch you ever did see, and for a long time it just sat there, and everyone noticed it. Then came a time when all kinds of things went wrong. One guy was more than just a little bit late with some pipe he'd promised to deliver. Brady sorely needed that pipe to finish his job. Another guy delivered something shoddy; a third, fourth, and even a fifth guy let Brady down, something that hadn't happened before. Now Brady did top work and demanded top work, top parts, with no exceptions. So he was sorely vexed with people letting him down. Still, Brady was a joking, kindly man, and so it was more in fun than in rage that he stuck some papers, papers with names on them, onto the thorn branch. Heck, maybe it was even bills sent by people who billed him in time but did not deliver in time, or did a job that had to be done over the right way, the people who can drive you broke. Yes, I believe Brady made a joke; "Here, these guys stuck me, now this old thorn branch is the place to stick their bills, drat and double drat!"

Anyway, on a Friday afternoon at quitting time, Brady stuck that thorn branch with more than one paper.

Monday morning somebody mentioned it over the coffee and doughnuts. That fellow, the one who delivered a load of pipe to Brady more than just a little bit late, more even than considerable late, and had delivered the wrong size pipe! Well sir, on Friday afternoon at quitting time that fellow had tripped over a piece of broken pipe. Broke his arm in two places, in such a little fall.

Hearing the news, Brady felt sorry for the guy, but his mind was occupied with wondering if now there would be more delay with the pipes he was awaiting. Brady never thought a thing about any connection to the thorn branch.

The following Friday it was, when someone else, another guy whose bill was on the thorn branch, drove his car into a tree, a tree that had been growing alongside the road for thirty years or more, a tree the guy did not see because of the fog that blinded him that Friday evening when he was going home from work. Brady heard about the accident, and the broken leg that laid the guy up, but he didn't connect the accident to the thorn branch.

Another week passed, and on a Friday night another guy who had a bill stuck on Brady's thorn branch, a guy who had driven Brady half-crazy with how he had set a fireplace all crooked in a house (Brady ripped the fireplace out with his own hands. Told the guy to do it over, and darned if the guy did not set it in crooked again!), that guy was swimming, got a cramp, nearly drowned. He was laid up with a pneumonia for weeks afterward. Well sir, everyone who worked for Brady knew about the thorn branch, and everyone had noticed the papers on the thorn branch, and there was some whispering going on in those parts. Let me tell you.

By the time Brady had put it together that three guys

whose names or bills were on thorns had had close calls of one sort or another, other people had been whispering for a while. About the time it occurred to Brady to notice the strange coincidences, he began to hear the whispers.

But, before he put it together, he *did* get delivery of those pipes! As a matter of fact, there was a time just before Brady heard the whispers and figured out what must be going on, well sir, there was a time when people treated Brady real good! He just said "please" and everybody jumped to it.

But Brady, as soon as he put it together, Brady took a long look at the thorn branch. Folks were always saying that Brady had survived being buried alive and that did make him a lucky man. Having *been* lucky was enough for Brady. He took the slips of paper off the thorn branch and threw them into the trash can. Brady had to pull on leather working gloves to carry the thorn branch; it was that spiky. Nobody knew where he took it. But Brady took it away.

He told me he was sure he got rid of the thorn branch just in time, before he found himself in real trouble. Out loud he called those accidents "coincidence," but to me he said a man would be a fool to use his good luck for revenge.

Well sir, it was a full thirty years later, and not so very long ago, that Brady was holding in his arms a lovely little child, a granddaughter barely one year old. There he stood, at the top of a long flight of cement stairs, holding that baby in his arms. He took the first step down that staircase. How Brady fell, nobody knows, but fall he did, clear to the bottom of those cement stairs, down to the cement floor. All the way down, Brady thought only that he had to protect the baby, had to hold her up safe. He did.

From the cement floor at the bottom of the stairs, Brady himself got up and moved carefully, stood the baby on her little feet. Something with his neck was not just right, so Brady and his wife did drive to the emergency room, Brady holding his head just so.

"Set still," ordered the doctor in the emergency room. "You are in luck, mister."

Brady, alive, agreed. In that tiny hospital in the middle of nowhere was a doctor who had run away from the big city to recover from a broken heart. That doctor had, in the big city, specialized in treating broken necks.

Old Brady said how good it was he had not wasted his luck on the thorns of that branch. ♦

"I DUNNO," Sidney said. "Sometimes having one tiny little thorn might not be a bad idea."

The old cowboy knocked his ashes out of his pipe on the heel of his boot, then put the pipe into his pocket and buttoned the flap.

"Unless the thorn pricks you." He winked at Sidney, who grinned.

At the door, he waved good-bye with his battered hat.

"Gee, it's dark outside," Sidney said.

"Yeah." Jeff checked his watch and the classroom clock: both said it was a quarter past ten; both had stopped for no apparent reason. He shrugged. "No matter what crazy time it is, it's time to mix the rayon fluff, time to sew the pillow covers. I wonder where the material is?"

"I can tell you a story," Eustace ventured. "About the time I was walking with my dog, Bengee, who was such a good dog that she walked along with me without a leash. 'Course, I had a leash in my hand, just in case a policeman or somebody would say something. And sure enough, a cop stopped me. 'Hey kid! How come that mutt's not leashed?' he demanded. Now I was sort of proud of Bengee and sort of showed off with her, how she'd stop and sit and all. And I told her stuff and she did it and then the policeman said in a very mean voice, 'Oh yeah, is she so good that she'll never attack, no matter if I hit her like this and this?' And he hit poor Bengee hard right and left with his gun, and she fell down and lay absolutely still. And I was crying and he said, laughing, 'Yeah, I guess she doesn't attack.' And I yelled at him, 'You're no police officer! My dad is a police officer and he would *never* do anything like that!' And then the guy laughed again and grabbed me. 'Right kid. I ain't no cop, and you're coming with me!' "

"Eustace, then what happened?" everyone asked.

"I don't know. I was crying and yelling so much that my dad came and woke me up."

"You mean that was a dream! What a crummy thing to do, telling us that!" Grace shouted.

"I feel cheated when a story, a book, or a movie turns out being only a dream!" Sidney said.

The whole class was shouting "yeah" at Eustace, when another visitor appeared at the door pretending to clear his throat.

"Ah-hem, ah-hem there, chaps. Wellington P. Wells, sometimes known as Dr. Wells of the Wells Famous Cures, a former orphan of this place, named for the well of pure spring water that is somewhere beneath this very school, educated in the orphanage here, sent out into the world, where I did indeed make my fortune. And where I have seen and do see and hear, and on occasion do, the most amazing things! Greetings, chaps!"

With a sort of dance-bow, the visitor came into the room. He certainly did look like someone in costume for *The Music Man,* with his tight-fitting suit, vest, his shirt with its high white collar, his plastered-down hair and the wire-rimmed glasses slipping down his nose, and, of course, his confident smile. Everyone stared at him, their arms elbow-deep in the rayon fluff.

"You may resume your work, chaps, while I tell you about one of my favorite people, a chap who lives not so very far from here, Jakey by name."

❖ Jakey's Best Bargains

Jakey had two great passions. The second was his collection of bumper stickers. Of that vast collection, his favorite was "Eat Road-Kills!" Of course, Jakey had other collections—baseball cards, comic books, little cars—but the bumper stickers were by far his best and most beloved collection.

It is not about his collections, but about Jakey's first and greatest passion that I want to tell you. You see, Jakey's first and greatest passion was *bargains:* bargains and, connected to bargains, entering all the contests that were offered in the mail. Jakey spent hours every day reading the entire contents of the "Grand Sweepstakes Prize!!! RUSH!!!!!" envelopes that arrived at his house. He spent hours more filling in the blanks, deciding whether or not to order whatever the sweepstakes company was selling. As a result of entering these contests, buying special offers, and shopping for bargains, and because of the prizes he kept on winning, Jakey had closets full of amazing objects, such as his set of genuine artistic pearl earrings and matching toenail decorations.

The first time Jakey received one of these wonderful

mail-order creations, he immediately realized that it would be perfect to give as a birthday gift. Jakey had many interesting and unusual gifts stored in his closets, ready for any gift-giving occasion. Jakey also had "half a dozen guaranteed genuine Swiss Army knives, sold for a total cost of *only* $2.13 in an extra-special, one-time-only offer!" True, the Swiss Army knives Jakey saw in the stores had handles of a somewhat shiny red plastic with a white Swiss cross on them, and the blades were sharp, shiny stainless steel. Jakey's genuine knives, when they arrived, were of a most interesting shade of dull purplish-orange plastic, each with a lopsided beige-gray cross on the handle. The blades? Well, no amount of charity could claim they were shiny or sharp. Jakey, who had rather been looking forward to having a fine Swiss Army knife at the end of his key chain, put them away in his closet of future gifts.

During an exceptionally long rainy spell one spring, Jakey discovered what he knew was going to be his all-time best bargain, and was he happy! While the rain drenched the world outside, Jakey had been poring over his mail, carefully reading all the special offers in the advertising circulars that choked his mailbox. There, on the very bottom of the pile, was a totally awesome offer: for a mere three dollars, Jakey could buy a LIFETIME SUBSCRIPTION to *Buyer's Delight*, a journal that promised exciting stories, thrilling articles, and plenty of how-to information for every wise and well-informed consumer seeking full value for his money. And the journal promised hours of entertainment monthly. Wow. Jakey couldn't wait to fill out the form and send away the three dollars.

In no time at all, the first issue arrived. Jakey carefully unfolded the somewhat limp newspaper. On the front page was a rather embarrassing article. It had the word "sex" four times in a sixteen-word headline. That article took up half the front page. The other half was occupied by an article on how to save money at the supermarket. The supermarket article was accompanied by a quiz. Jakey answered all the questions, and then turned the paper upside down to see what kind of shopper he was. The quiz revealed that he was "wise and careful."

Inside, on page two, were the how-to articles. There was one on repairing leaking faucets, one on building skateboard ramps, one on removing splinters, and one on how to give yourself a haircut. All of the articles were illustrated with drawings and diagrams.

Page two also had an interview with a man who said there was a spaceship parked in his garden. A fuzzy photograph of what looked like a greatly pitted pancake on very much enlarged grass accompanied the article, which also said that the occupants of the spaceship had held a cookout in the man's garden. For the cookout, the man said, the spaceship occupants had roasted and eaten the man's pet cat. When the man protested, the spaceship visitors had asked him if he wanted to give them dessert or *be* their dessert.

Page three had a recipe column at the top of the page. It gave four recipes for tuna casserole. The first was with potatoes and corn chips, the second with rice and corn flakes, the third with noodles and potato chips, and the fourth, which was called Nuvelle Tuna Aloha, combined tuna with canned pineapple and fresh kiwi, and was decorated with sliced peaches and dill pickles. Jakey liked tuna, so he cut out the recipes so that he could try them one by one.

At the bottom of the page was a large and complex crossword puzzle all about diseases advertised on TV and the remedies for them that also were advertised on TV. Jakey finished the puzzle the day the paper arrived and felt very proud of himself. Page four had an article about places to write for free brochures, free samples, and free catalogs. Jakey wrote to all of them. It took days, and lots of stamps, but the flood of mail in return made Jakey very happy. Some of the places even sent bumper stickers.

Page four also had a chart telling how to remove bubble gum from pillow cases and sheets, from the hair on one's head, from shirts and furniture. Jakey cut out the chart to save it. Jakey was indeed delighted with his LIFETIME SUBSCRIPTION to *Buyer's Delight* and looked forward to the next issue.

As the offer had promised, exactly one month later the second issue of *Buyer's Delight* arrived. Trembling with excitement, Jakey unfolded the paper to the front page. On it appeared the very same how-to articles with the very same diagrams and drawings that had been on page two of the previous issue. The article with the word "sex" appearing four times in the sixteen-word headline was on page three of the second issue. The same crossword puzzle Jakey had already solved was on page one, the same tuna recipes on page four. Truly mystified, Jakey put the newspaper into the recycling bin and waited for the next month to bring a new copy of *Buyer's Delight*.

In the issue that arrived the following month, the interview with the man who had a spaceship parked in his garden had been moved to page one; all the other articles had been moved. There were no new articles. Jakey knew the old articles by heart. To make matters worse, the newspaper was so limp that it was useless for making paper airplanes or for wrapping the garbage; even the recycling man said he didn't want to see it. Jakey felt cheated. Every month when the paper arrived, it was a reminder that he had paid a whole three dollars for a LIFETIME SUBSCRIPTION, and now that darned paper would come to his mailbox every month for the rest of his life.

Sending three dollars for that subscription had been a big mistake; thinking of it made Jakey very gloomy indeed. Still, every month, Jakey opened the paper, always hoping it would truly change. For eleven whole months Jakey was disappointed; but with the twelfth issue, Jakey got his reward. There, on the front page, was a completely new article, and a very special offer.

For a mere four dollars Jakey could remove his name from the LIFETIME SUBSCRIPTION list of *Buyer's Delight* and never, ever receive another copy.

Without hesitation, Jakey paid.♦

DURING THE TELLING of his story, Dr. Wellington P. Wells had seated himself on the corner of Ms. Laurel's desk. As he concluded, he made a rather sweeping bow to a full round of applause by the class. Walking around to the back of the desk, he sat down in Ms. Laurel's chair, and leaning forward, peered over his spectacles at the class. Everyone stared at him expectantly, but he just stared back at them.

After a very long minute, Tilly blurted out, "Are you a ghost?"

"Ha-ha! You blinked first!" Wells shouted. "I win."

"But we didn't know it was a staring contest," Jeff protested.

"Still," said Wells, "I win . . . and some prefer the word 'shade.' After all, I am a mere shadow of my former self. Get it? Shadow, shade!" He leaned back in the chair, laughing, clearly pleased with his wit.

"It wasn't that funny," someone grumbled.

"Shhh!" said Jeff. "He's our guest." Then turning to Dr. Wells, Jeff asked, "You prefer the word 'shade?'"

"No. I merely said it to make my little joke. If asked to answer seriously, I'd say I am a memory. I remember this place and it remembers me. At this time, however, there is a veritable whirlwind of memories, of earth spirits and others, all drawn to this place."

"Will they all stay here when the building goes?"

"Some may. I don't know." He sighed. "Yes, nice to pass the time with you chaps." With a small yawn, he folded his arms on Ms. Laurel's desk, pillowed his head on them, and went to sleep.

One by one, just as if they had been napping kindergartners lulled by his example, all of them fell asleep.

When they awoke, Wells was gone, the room dark.

Jeff stretched, stood up, stretched again, then began filling the canvas bags with rayon fluff. "I guess this stuff has been mixed enough," he mumbled aloud.

"Yeah," Grace and Sidney agreed.

"Sooo dark," said Eustace, "and all those clocks, so crazy."

Beyond the line of fir trees at the edge of the school yard, a cold, bright quarter moon shone. The fir trees' shadows, long and straight, pointed toward the school.

A faint light glimmered in the hall. Gathering up the materials of their work, Jeff, Sidney, Grace, Eustace, and the others moved like sleepwalkers toward what appeared to be the source of the light, the staircase leading down to the library. No one spoke; no one ran ahead or lagged behind. Approaching the library, they could see light and shadows moving, as if there were a fire in there. Certainly there was the smell of wood smoke. Upon reaching the doorway, they could see that, yes, it was fire, a huge fire in a gigantic fireplace that stood where the check-out desk should be. To the right and left of them, in the darkness, they could see the shadows of what had been the usual library tables and bookcases, things that had been carted away hours ago!

But in the fireplace were hooks for hanging kettles, metal skewers for roasting meats, the door to an oven. In front of the fireplace stood a great long table, its surface smooth and bare. Back in the shadows was another table, perhaps a cabinet. They moved closer for a better look. Except for the crackling of the fire, the room was silent. Over on the cabinet, they could see a basket of eggs, another containing carrots, onions, turnips, and parsley, green and wet, on top.

"I am very, very hungry," said Jeff. "Whatever is happening is weird, but it seems to be for us; so I suggest we make ourselves something to eat."

"I feel as if I've been here before," Felton said. "I don't know but I feel comfortable." He carried the vegetables to the table. "Wish I knew where they had gone, and if we need to help them."

"Ms. Oakes?" Grace asked, bringing the eggs.

"All of them, Ms. Holly, Ms. Oakes, and Ms. Laurel," said Sidney.

The cabinet held knives and a flour bin. On a low bench next to the wall stood four buckets of clean water, on the floor a pail for scrapings. A crock of butter, a wooden spoon with an enormously long handle. One by one the means were found, and they set to work cleaning vegetables and cutting them. Into the kettle they put the butter and the vegetables, stirring all the while. When Grace took up the cabbage, someone protested.

"Not in the soup?" she asked. "Okay, then cabbage salad." And she set to slicing.

"Noodles," declared Felton, "we need noodles. I'll make them!"

At once everyone protested; everyone wanted to make noodles, even though it meant they would have noodles and vegetables rather thick together and not a soup at all.

Jeff poured water into the kettle of vegetables, thereby producing steam with a fine aroma. The salt crock was found, the soup salted. Everyone put a mound of flour on the table. Everyone got an egg. Into the flour went the egg, which was followed by careful stirring; then the dough was flattened out, which was done with hands patting it down for lack of rolling pins. While the noodles dried, the children looked for bowls, but at first found only a single large one, which Grace took for her cabbage salad. When Sidney and Eustace rumaged in a cupboard back in the dark part of the room, they found bowls, spoons, vinegar, and oil.

"No fair eating raw dough!" Grace shouted at Sidney, who had pinched a good-sized piece from the drying noodles.

Before the vegetables were fully cooked, the noodles went into the broth. The table got scrubbed and set, and people began to demand, one after the other, "Is it ready yet?"

As the last bowl was being carried to the table, a voice from the shadows wished them good appetite.

Jeff did jump at the sound, but without even spilling very much of the soup, he managed a "thank you" as he set the bowl on the table.

"Are you a shade, or . . . ah . . . a memory, too?" someone asked.

"No," said the voice. They could see it was a girl, older than they, when she stepped into the light. Straight, thick brown hair hung down to her waist. She wore jeans and a shirt, and was barefoot. "I'm quite real, and very hungry. Do you have enough for me?" Her voice was light with laughter, her manner rather shy.

"Sure. There's even a bowl and spoon. Here."

"Thank you," she said.

The noodles and vegetables were served, and the girl joined them at the table.

"Bless this food!" Eustace cried. "And all you guys, and me, too!"

In the minutes that followed, they ate quietly, giggling occasionally when a noodle slipped off a spoon. Trying not to stare, at least not obviously, they studied the girl. Her eyebrows were straight, very thick, very black as she looked down at her bowl. When it was empty, she praised their cooking, but declined their offer of seconds, saying, "You asked if I am a shade, which I am not. . . . I am not of this place, nor have I ever been . . . but there *is* more to tell."

❖ On Meeting Witches at Wells

I live alone, entirely by my own choice, high on a remote mountain lake. The water in my lake is fine for swimming, canoeing, or sailing. It is excellent for fishing. I use the water for cooking and washing, but I do not drink it. The water in my lake has a disease in it, one we call Beaver Fever. The name offends the beavers. I don't even know if the fever makes them sick. Certainly bears, deer, otters, and others drink the water, but humans become ill.

Actually, the name offends only some of the beavers; others say it's better to be known for the fever than not to be known at all. It's a question to ponder.

Nevertheless, I drive from my little lakeside house across a ridge with alpine meadows on both sides, then down a wooded road to a little spring. Yes, we call it a spring rather than a well because the water has come up on its own rather than by humans digging down. In a tiny open space full of long grasses and wildflowers swaying in the breeze, there stands a tiny shack, its wood silver with age. From the shack comes the sound of water bubbling up from the ground. The person who built the shack to protect the purity of the water has done further work to make it possible for us to take the water. If you bend down and peer into a hole in the wall of the shack at the place where the pipe comes out, you can see a large ceramic ring, which has been placed on the ground where the water comes up from the earth. The water bubbles up, fills the ring and spills over the edges to form a rivulet that runs into a larger stream. On top of the ring rests an iron pipe. As the water runs over the rim, a sufficient quantity flows through the pipe and out of the silver shed. Those of us who wish to drink the water may fill our jugs or cups at the pipe, or simply lean over to sip the icy water as it flows.

Now, I am the third and youngest sister, and I have been raised on the proper etiquette for meeting witches and been told what can happen if one is rude, and what tests witches may put to girls and boys. I know these things, and I know, too, that wells and springs have always been places of powerful magic, places where one is most likely to meet with witches. I know that it is wise to be well-behaved, always.

The recent summer day on which I went to fill my two jugs at the spring was a glorious day indeed. The sun was warm, the breezes gentle, the sky a blue of such purity you could taste it. There were orange Indian paintbrush blooming in swaying masses beside the road, and more kinds of daisies than you could dream. Butterflies of velvet brown and pale blue played tag in and out of the shade.

I arrived to find a large, squat black truck parked at the entrance to the path that goes from the road to the spring. A pasty boy, sweating and sullen, pushed two plastic bottles with labels on them that said "liquid bleach" across the bed of the truck. To my "good morning" he grunted, then walked, head down, ahead of me on the path.

At the spring stood the two largest women I had ever seen. One was gray and old, with just a single tooth in her head. Her thin hair was wound in greasy rollers. Her blouse, which did not meet across her middle, was missing many buttons. She spat into the stream when I greeted her. A third woman, far, far larger than the other two, sat on a huge plastic container. Its markings declared it held the sweet syrup to make a soda fountain drink. I shuddered to think how many gallons of pure drinking water that syrup had polluted. The sandy clearing next to the shack was entirely covered with plastic containers of all colors and sizes. I counted fifty.

As they filled the containers, the three quarreled. Occasionally, as if to change the pace, they called the sweating boy "stupid," "lazy," or "dummy." The old one spoke in a whine, which the boy echoed in his responses. The one who sat on the syrup container lit one cigarette after another, tossing matches and the finished butts into the stream, on the waving grass, or on the sand at our feet.

I waited patiently. Gradually I struck up a conversation with the boy, asking him what grade he'd finished that year in school, about his summer vacation. His responses were gloomy, completely without hope. The women glared at me, at my clean shirt, at my feet, bare in the sand of the path. The one who smoked while she filled the containers was vain, admiring her hands, with their long, pointed nails painted brilliant crimson, every time she flicked her cigarette or screwed the cap onto another jug. Patiently I waited.

I waited while they filled, and smoked, and complained, and criticized everyone and everything. I waited while they stared at me with loathing. I waited patiently and courteously as I had been taught.

But then a truck stopped on the other side of the road, and a young man got out. He had obviously been working very hard. His hair, face, neck, and shirt were wet with sweat. In his hand he held a small bottle. Seeing the women, and me waiting with my two bottles, he hesitated. The three ignored him, prepared that he should wait until they had done the last of their fifty jugs, until they had filled the final one on which the cruelest of the women still reposed her great bulk. We were expected to wait.

As that woman took a jug away from the pipe, before she could put another in its place, I quickly stepped forward. Smiling first at the women and then at the young man, I said to him, "Here. Please don't be shy. Take a drink. You must want to soak your head, to cool yourself after your hard work." Blushing, he smiled back at me, thanked the women, and bent to the iron pipe. He drank, wet his neckerchief, filled his small bottle, then stepped away so that he would not impede the women's progress. With a slight bow, he turned and went back up the path, got into his truck, and drove away.

The women glared at me until he had left, and then began to berate me. "How dare you stick your nose into our water. You'll make us late!" "You have your nerve! We ought to teach you a lesson!"

At that, I lost all patience with them and stamped my foot. One, two, three, four times.

Done!

There, blinking in the sunshine, stood three huge green frogs, and one small brown one. Certainly they were all much more attractive in that form than they had been as humans. Then, suddenly, one of the bigger frogs began to menace the little brown one. Taking pity on that poor earth-bound boy, I decided that he had suffered enough from those three women. With a word, I made him an osprey instead. He flew above my head in a circle, crying, and again I pitied him and turned their squat black truck into another osprey, mate and friend for him.

Those many plastic jugs I turned into translucent white stones. They looked so pretty in the golden sand of the path and stream. Then, carefully, I picked up each and every filthy cigarette butt and sodden match and put them into the trash can that the considerate builder of the silver spring house had provided. When I had finished filling my two jugs and drunk my fill of sweet, clear water, I turned to look once more at the clearing. A dozen velvet-brown and blue butterflies played tag in and out of the shadows, as three green frogs hopped off in search of flies.♦

"**GOOD FOR YOU.**" Felton beamed. "Did you come here to save the school?"

"No. There's no saving," said the girl with long hair. "I came to see all of you. It isn't in evil, not in anger either, that the spring is taking back this place for its own. I know that Laurel, Oakes, and Holly are sad, because they have loved the school for so long. You need to finish the pillows, while I try to bring the three of them away from the spring. I think they are brooding."

"They're down under the school somewhere?" Jeff stared at the floor, half expecting it to open at his feet.

"Yes. I want to bring them up and out so they can help you, and leave this place when the time comes."

"Soon?" asked Tilly.

"I don't know."

"Where's the material for the covers? And what are we gonna do for needles and thread?" Jeff pointed to the bags of rayon fluff alongside the door.

"You don't have the material yet?"

"No. But Ms. Oakes said she was going to see about it. If she, or someone, doesn't bring it, we could look for whatever scraps of cloth might be in the art room. Unless the movers took everything."

Sidney grabbed a canvas bag and took off down the hall.

"Wait!" Jeff, followed by the others, was three steps behind her.

The first door to the art/crafts/shop room was stuck shut. No matter how they pushed, they could not open it. Barton ran to the supply closet, which also led into the classroom. That door was unlocked. Once they were inside the room, they could see that four sewing machines had been covered with moving blankets and stacked on a dolly, which stood, with its wheels locked, against the door they had been unable to open. Putting down the canvas bags, they picked up the machines, a kid holding each end, and carried them back to the places where they had originally stood. Jeff tried the electricity, which worked. Three other sewing machines had been left in place.

Four bags of wildly colored fabric leaned against two cupboards, which the kids opened to find more stacks of cloth inside. Drawers of scissors, needles, and thread were stacked beside empty cabinets.

"Looks as if the movers started and then left," Eustace remarked, testing the thread on one of the machines. "All seven machines work. I say we take turns; sew three sides on the machine. Some people stuff the pillows, and the rest sew them shut. Man. This material for the covers hurts your eyes, it's so bright."

"Yeah," said Jeff, "not the usual gray cloth they used when my dad made his. So much for tradition."

"Yeah. Wish we had a radio. How much time do you think we have?"

"I don't know."

"Naw. You don't need a radio. I have something better." The guy standing by the windows was huge, muscles on his muscles, his jaws working a wad of gum the size of your fist. Sidney watched him with real longing. Who knew how many hours had really passed since she had so foolishly thrown away her own bubble gum? The guy slouched against the radiator, hands in the pockets of his high school football jacket, which he wore open over a tight T-shirt.

"See," he continued, "I came to hang out with you guys, and to tell you a love story. . . ." He grinned when they laughed. "Honest. It's a real love story. Just listen. . . ."

❖ The Silver Skier

There was Keith, the new kid in the high school, the first day of school. There was Keith, a guy who did not believe in love at first sight, not even when he saw Marcy and *became* a guy in love at first sight!

Marcy was the perfect girl in his eyes, athletic, funny, smart, a girl full of life. Keith's wonderful dumb luck was that Marcy liked him, too. Those months that followed were so cool, so smooth. Her parents liked him; his parents loved her. There were so many great possibilities ahead. Life looked terrific. They talked about life, about college, about *where* they wanted to live, about *how*, about all the things that were important to them. The school, the work, the sports, everything was sweet. Marcy's parents had been in love since high school, married after college, married thirty years, with Marcy their youngest. They had no problem at all with kids who were "serious."

When winter came, Keith got all excited about the snow. He'd moved from a place that was mild in the winter, and now there would be all that wonderful, deep white stuff, and all the winter sports. Keith wanted badly to learn to ski, and had saved money just so he could take lessons. If he worried about anything, it was that Marcy, having grown up there with all that great snow, would laugh over her shoulder at him while she hotdogged it and he sweated the snowplow.

Marcy was standing in front of the bulletin board, talking with a bunch of their best friends, when Keith saw the first ski club notice pinned up on the board. "Oh great! Terrific!" he beamed. "I wanna join the ski club, take lessons, go skiing with you. I know when you outski me I'll be bumming. But just wait, I'll catch up!"

As he spoke, Marcy got all white, excused herself, and walked away, just as if she didn't want to talk to him. Keith, completely bewildered, looked at the others. Nobody met his eyes. "What's wrong?"

Nobody answered. They just walked away from him. Poor old Keith was left staring at the bulletin board.

Later, when he tried asking Marcy, she shook her head and changed the subject. Still later, he asked Marcy's best friend, Abby, who looked at him a long time before she replied. "You like to joke a lot. Sure you aren't joking now? You really don't know?"

"No. Heck. I don't know. I don't even know what I don't know," Keith protested. "C'mon, Abby. What's up?"

"Until last year," she began, "Marcy was competing, racing, in skiing. She looked good as a possible Olympic contender. It was the last day of a ski weekend, a terrific trip. It was late in the afternoon. If we hurried, we could make one last run before the lifts closed. Marcy, running ahead of the rest of us, was alone when she got to the lifts. She got into a chair, and then some dude in a silver ski suit—the one-piece kind that snowmobilers wear—skied up and got onto the double chair with her. I saw them way ahead of us. What happened next, I only know part of. . . . But Marcy fell on her way down, skiing fast, as if she wanted to get away from that guy. When we got to her, he was gone. Then she was sick, feverish, for weeks. Now she won't even say the word 'ski.'"

"You think that guy said something? Tried something?" Keith demanded, angry at the thought of the guy.

"I don't know. But, please, don't say anything about what I told you, anything about skiing, to Marcy. She really can't take it!"

Keith completely stopped talking about skiing, but he could not stop wanting to go. So he did. He went off alone, took lessons, and enjoyed skiing more than he had imagined.

Then, when he got the chance, he talked alone with Marcy's father. "Do you think Marcy will get over this not wanting to ski?"

Marcy's father did not answer right away. He seemed to be trying to make up his mind about something. Keith waited, feeling more and more uncomfortable, as if he were in for something not at all to his liking.

"Look, Keith," Marcy's father began, then stopped,

then began again. "My theory is that Marcy was coming down with something, some virus, that day when she went skiing. You know, sometimes you feel the absolute best, most terrific, splendid in fact, just hours before you get sick with something that lays you flat. I think that as the fever came on, Marcy hallucinated, but what she told us was that some fellow in a silver ski outfit sat himself beside her on the chair lift. On the ride up, he struck her as a conceited bore. He boasted of his skiing, said a guy as handsome as he could only have for his girl the most beautiful girl, the best skier, and that lucky Marcy had been chosen by him for that honor. She said his vanity was incredible, disgusting. He went on about mussing his hair, how the wind must not muss his hair and how he did not want to get 'hat head.' As they skied off the lift, he said that now they would play tag, and he'd catch her. She would be his. As he said it, he took off his head and tucked it under his arm. She said that from under his arm his head was still talking, while he skied after her."

"Ridiculous!" said Keith.

"Exactly," replied Marcy's father. "Later I made inquiries. I was never able to find anyone on the staff of the resort who'd seen that silver fellow. Me, I think that Marcy was feverish. But now Marcy says she knows that man is waiting for her, wherever she goes to ski. She thinks he will carry her off. She is terrified. Whether her fear will diminish with time, whether she will ski again, I cannot say. We have decided not to push her."

"No, no," said Keith. "I don't want to push her."

For all the rest of that long winter, Keith avoided all mention of skiing when he was with Marcy or any of their friends. He did continue to go off for lessons on his own, because he kept picturing the two of them together on a snowy slope, cutting beautiful tracks downhill, then the two of them on the lift swinging up over the trees. With that dream, which he kept to himself, Keith went through that winter and into spring.

The following school term opened with Marcy and Keith seniors and still serious about one another and about their future together.

By the time ski season rolled around, Keith felt so sure of his love of Marcy, of how the two of them could face anything together, that he slowly began to nudge Marcy toward the slopes. He nudged and he nagged and he cajoled and he promised he would not leave her side, and he painted rosy pictures of college ski trips, of how he and she would someday take their children skiing. In short, he convinced Marcy that no guy in a silver ski suit could possibly be a threat to her, not now, not with Keith at her side. Keith had convinced Marcy and himself.

The day Marcy and Keith went skiing was splendid indeed. They skied a beautiful mountain, not the one where Marcy had suffered her, shall we say, "unfortunate experience."

Keith's lessons and practice, and Marcy's lack of practice, made them about an even match. The day went well, until there was time for just one more run. Together, holding hands, they skied up to the double chair. Together, holding hands, they rode the gently swaying chair up the mountain, high over the evergreen forest, over the trails wide and narrow. At the top station, they skied down off the chair, not pausing as they began their run, Keith feeling proud that he could run close, right in Marcy's tracks.

The skier, a tall guy in a silver ski suit, coming fast, knocked Keith down hard. With one hand, the skier in the silver suit picked Marcy up right off the trail and carried her away. His head, with its perfect blond curls, was tucked under his other arm, talking all the while, telling Marcy how patiently he'd waited for her. Keith could not hear him of course, and neither could he hear Marcy. Her scream was silent, but Keith could feel it, in the place where his heart had been, before he fell in love at first sight. ♦

''OH MY GOSH,'' whispered Grace. "Couldn't Keith go after them and save her?"

"I dunno." The muscular guy shrugged. "I only heard it from my big brother. Well, see ya." And he was gone.

With a shudder, they all got back to work. Each sewed five cases, and then let someone else have a turn on the machine. They took turns stuffing, sewing ends, and packing pillows into whatever canvas bags they had.

It got to be Jeff's turn. *This is great,* he thought. The machine rocketed along, sewing one seam after another, Jeff humming as they went. Lost in his own thoughts, in watching the material move under the needle, Jeff jumped right off the chair when he heard someone singing, running through the scales, in a voice so powerful it made the windows of the classroom rattle. When he looked around, he saw that he was not the only one to be a bit undone by the singing. The rest of the kids stared, mouths open, at the place where the muscular guy had been standing a few minutes ago.

"Sorry," the visitor said, singing the words. "I am small but I have a very big voice, and I was just keeping it warm. You see, I came here, clear from New Jersey, because old Ron, "Big Ron" we call him at our school, told you that old silver skier story, and I didn't want you to mess up your sewing because you had to keep looking over your shoulders to see what might be behind you."

At her words, everyone did turn around to look into the dark corners of the classroom. The girl laughed, a sort of singing trill. "Would you like to hear," she stopped talking to run through the scales again, "a different sort of story?"

"Sure, it was only that with your voice and the windows rattling, we jumped because we're expecting something, we aren't sure what, to take this building . . ." He shrugged. ". . . take it somewhere . . ."

"Yes, I know, so I suppose I should begin."

"Excuse me?" Grace hesitated. "Did you and Big Ron go to this school?"

"Our grandmothers did. We still have their story pillows, kinda worn, but full of good stuff." She giggled. "I want to tell you about someone at our school. . . ."

❖ Flute at the Gasoline Pump

Without exception, every kid in school loves Flute! She is kind and funny, and . . . But first I should tell you the "not becauses."

Flute is not called Flute because her voice is high and thin. Her voice is low and soft.

She is not called Flute because she plays the flute; it's one of the few instruments she does not play. Piano and especially the organ are Flute's main instruments.

She's not called Flute because it in any way rhymes with or reflects upon her own real name, except that "Flute" fits her — and her own real last name has thirteen syllables.

Flute teaches choir in our school, and she is a terrific teacher. The kids feel they are learning. Furthermore, they sing beautifully, and thereby show they've learned. The choirs in the school are big and varied, all taught by Flute and her sidekick/codirector, the two of them seeming to be in five places at once.

What you gotta know is that the love the kids feel for Flute comes about not only because she is a good teacher, and a kind person, and a respected, world-class musician. No way. You see, we love her because the same terrible, nightmare-but-in-real-life things happen to Flute as happen to all us kids. She is forever the victim of the very same sorts of disasters you and I dread. You know how terrible, embarrassing things happen. You feel twice miserable: first because they happen, and second because something tells you that somehow you could have, should have, avoided them, and yet . . . Well, here, I'll tell you how it is.

On a typical morning, Flute comes to class and sees all the kids sitting there depressed, miserable in all that humiliates them in reality and in their imaginations. Flute immediately tells of her disasters, and while she tells, everybody laughs, as she intends for us to do. We laugh until the tears flow, and we hug her, and then we sing. And then, after school, we go home and tell the whole family, and everyone feels, "Ahh, there but for the grace of God go I."

Flute, out of some sense of need for protection from the forces of the world, drives an enormous automobile. It is huge, and gets about a mile and a half per gallon of gasoline when it is efficiently sailing down the highways. Not too many weeks ago, Flute drove that monster car from New Jersey, where she lives, to Pennsylvania for a recording session. Flute had been asked to play a particular organ in a particular church. All afternoon, Flute had played magnificently on that church organ, and the recording session had gone smoothly.

Nevertheless, it had been a long recording session. It was after dark when Flute gathered up her music, her handbag, and her car keys and walked out of the church. There, in the church parking lot, under quite a bit of snow, sat Flute's large automobile. The snow was still falling. Flute brushed the snow off the car windows.

She had a decision to make. That snow falling was not a small flurry. It was a storm. The recording engineers came out of the church saying that it would be snowing all night. Flute could simply clean off her car and start the long drive home. She did, however, have a standing invitation to dinner and to spend the night with friends who lived quite close to that church. Flute, who has always disliked driving in snowstorms, could telephone her husband at home in New Jersey to tell him about the storm. He, protective of Flute's safety, would surely urge her to remain in Pennsylvania until the storm had passed. Whatever she did, Flute needed to buy gasoline for the large automobile. It could never make it home, not tonight, not tomorrow, on what remained in the tank. Furthermore, it was her habit never to drive that car in bad weather with anything less than a full tank of gasoline.

Flute drove out of the church parking lot to look for a gas station that would be open at night in the storm. With the gasoline indicator flicking up and down around the "Empty" line, Flute finally discovered the only open gas station for miles. She could see immediately that it was one of those futuristic stations, with one very young boy locked up in a glass house and all the pumps standing in rows, unattended. Windshield wipers heavy with snow, tires slipping on the sloppy pavement, Flute drove her monster machine up next to a pump. She got out of the car and picked her way carefully through the deep snow over to the boy in the glass box.

"Hullo," said Flute timidly.

"C'n I help you?" replied the boy.

"I need to fill my tank," ventured Flute, "but I don't know how."

"You're from Jersey!" grinned the boy. "I can always tell. Nobody from Jersey knows how to fill a tank. It's against the law there?"

"I think so," said Flute, whose hands were beginning to freeze while she stood outside the glass box. "Please, can you fill it for me?"

"No," said the boy. "I can't leave this room until my relief gets here. It'll be soon, though. You could wait. But look; it's easy. I'll tell you how, and you can do it."

Flute was not at all sure it would be easy, but she nodded tentatively.

"First ya give me twenty dollars. It'll take about that much for your car. When you're done, I'll give you the change."

Flute nodded. With freezing fingers, she fumbled a twenty-dollar bill from her wallet and slid it into a tray at the bottom of the glass where the boy sat.

"Ya go over," he continued cheerfully, "take off the gas

cap. Pick up the hose; push the handle on the side of the pump down. Then, put the nozzle into the tank of your car. When you squeeze the handle, the gas will go. If you squeeze hard, the gas will flow until the tank is just full enough and then click off automatically. Got that?"

Flute nodded.

Flute walked through the ever-deepening snow to her car, repeating the instructions to herself. Cap. Turn thing on side. Squeeze.

The first problem arose because Flute's hands were so cold, and so was the gas cap. It was hard to get it off. Then, once it was off, it was also down. Three times she dropped the cap into the snow at her feet. Finally, just as Flute managed to get the gas cap to rest in the snow on the top of her car, a truck pulled up on the other side of the row of pumps.

As Flute walked carefully over to her gasoline pump, a handsome young man jumped out of the driver's side of the truck and waved a greeting to the boy in the glass booth. Walking toward his pump, the handsome young man touched the truck lovingly as he went. Looking again at the truck, Flute could understand why; it was spanking new, shining clean, polished, gleaming, with hardly any snow on it. An older woman sat in the truck's passenger seat. Ah, thought Flute, who is always tender-hearted, it's probably his mother. Flute smiled at them.

Bravely Flute turned the handle on the pump. With determination, she took out the nozzle and tried to walk away from the pump with it. The hose was so stiff, so heavy, so awkward. Flute heaved with all her strength, trying to maneuver the hose so that she could use it correctly.

Flute was trying to go to her car, to place the nozzle into her tank—but why was there an arc of gasoline coming out of the nozzle? Why was gasoline flowing like a fountain? And why was it pouring down on to the brilliantly shining truck standing on the other side of the pumps? And that handsome young man, the owner of the truck, he was staring at the arc of flowing gasoline with the same look of horrified amazement that Flute could feel on her own face. In her horror at what that gasoline was doing to the beautiful finish of that beautiful truck, Flute dropped the nozzle. The gasoline flow stopped.

Then. Then Flute knew that she must have caused the gasoline to flow. She must have squeezed the something. "Oh, I'm so sorry. So sorry!" Flute exclaimed to the handsome young man, and to the older woman who must be his mother, a woman who turned upon Flute a look of purest hatred. "Ohhh," said Flute, "I can wash it off." Slipping and sliding, she ran toward the boy in the glass booth. He had covered his face with his hands; his body was shaking with the laughter he tried to suppress.

"Could we—could I use some water?" she asked.

Without raising his face, the boy in the booth pointed to a bucket near the gas pumps. Flute took up a sponge and

shing off the truck. The handsome young man
ther sponge, but then stopped. As they put the
s onto the truck, the water froze. The sponges stuck
e roof of the beautiful truck. When Flute, frantic,
ed her sponge off, shreds of sponge remained frozen on
e spot. The handsome young man, looking stricken,
jumped back into his truck, started the engine, and sped
away.

Flute fumbled for the cap to her gas tank, screwed it into
place, then stumbled to the glass booth. Inside, the boy
still had his face in his hands.

"Please," whispered Flute, tapping lightly on the glass,
"please. I don't want any gasoline. Please could I have my
money back? Please, I just want to leave."

"I'm sorry," replied the boy, struggling to compose his
face, "but . . . but . . . ." He sighed. "I'm afraid you owe me
twenty-six cents for the . . . ," he swallowed hard, "for the
gasoline you used." ♦

GRACE RAN OVER to the tiny girl singer. "Can
you give Flute a hug from us?"

"Sure."

"But," Grace hesitated, "are you a shade, or a memory,
or a dream?"

"Me, a dream?" sang the girl. "Oh no. I think that I am
dreaming you guys." She hugged Grace and the others
who followed her, murmuring, "Yeah, Flute!"

8 6

"Good luck!" the tiny girl with the big voice said, and disappeared.

"Good luck yourself!" Jeff shouted after her, then resumed driving the sewing machine. This one was his very last pillow. Before he could announce it, however, he heard a series of ah-hems, a genteel clearing of throat, from above his head. Jeff looked up to see the old lady, the one in the cardigan who had been in Ms. Oakes's office at the beginning of the day. She looked different now. Her hair was fluffy, snowy white like a cloud around her face. She had a cane, which she held upside down, the crook caught onto the chair beside Jeff's machine. The old lady was holding on for dear life, as if only the cane kept her from floating away.

"Hello," Jeff said. "You look different."

"It's my hair," she replied. "It's gone all light, lifting me clear away." She sighed. "Nice pillows. Nice."

"Yeah," said Jeff, racing the machine around the last case. "This is the last one. Some of the other kids have started stuffing them. I know that in the old days the whole pillow was sewn by hand, but we'd never finish them unless we used the machines. We've been closing them with a seam sewn by hand."

"Oh yes," said the old lady. "You have done it correctly, with one seam sewn by hand. Those stories inside have to have some breath of fresh air. Do the last seam by hand. I'll keep you company. Anyway, can all of you hear me? I've come back again to tell you another story."

"Yo! Guys!" Jeff called to the others. "Can you all hear?" Everybody could, and so the old lady began.

"A long, long time ago." The old lady smiled, sighed, holding fast to her cane, her tiny black boots a good meter above the floor. "Ah-hemmm," clearing her throat once more, she continued . . .

❖ An Old, Often Retold, Story of Revenge

More than one hundred years ago, Mr. Malvern Bitterwood went to China to conduct his business. Bitterwood, an Englishman with a mustache, whiskers, and hair of a deep copper color, was a confirmed bachelor with definite ideas about how his life should be conducted. Thus, it was in short order that he had secured for himself a modest house in which to live, a house within a brisk walk of the place in which he would do his business. After arranging for the house, Mr. Bitterwood went into the market and purchased, for a few pennies, a servant. He was careful to choose a woman, not a young girl, one that to his mind was plain. Mr. Bitterwood wanted no one to have any incorrect ideas about the relationship between master and slave. Perhaps the seller attempted to show Bitterwood that the woman had sound teeth. Bitterwood took no notice of her hands and feet, whether they were large and coarse from work, or small and smooth. Leading his purchase home, Bitterwood put her into a dreary room beside the kitchen of his house. The room had one window up close to the ceiling, a window too small for even a child to crawl through. Window or no window, the young woman could not have escaped. All the town knew she had been purchased by the red devil of a foreigner.

Bitterwood, who would have no heathenish names in his house, called the servant Rose, and, over time, taught her how he wished his life to be conducted.

Before dawn she rose to heat water so that Bitterwood could wash himself and shave himself on those parts of his face near the mustache and beard. That hot water she carried upstairs in two large jugs. On her return trip downstairs, she took with her the chamber pot from Bitterwood's room. She emptied it of night soil; Rose then washed, dried, and returned the pot to its place.

She prepared Bitterwood's breakfast of fruit, boiled egg, smoked fish, and toast. She prepared and served hot coffee, the one luxury Malvern Bitterwood permitted himself.

Her days were spent caring for Bitterwood's house. With her own two hands and the soap she made, Rose boiled and scrubbed the table linens, bed linens, the shirts, shorts, and socks that Bitterwood wore. With her own two hands she prepared the starch; she sprinkled and ironed. Bitterwood taught her how much starch to use. Once he threw at her head two shirts that had too little, and once a shirt that had too much.

Rose cleaned and brushed and pressed his suits and waistcoats, his hats and gloves. She went to the market, purchased food, and prepared it. She kept the house clean and tidy, and made beside it a garden so graceful and serene that even Mr. Malvern Bitterwood came to appreciate it.

After breakfast, Bitterwood went to his business. Early in the afternoon he returned home for the midday meal. That meal ended with coffee, a cigar, a brief rest, and the walk back to his place of business. Most evenings, he returned home for supper, and occasionally went out afterward to enjoy a game of whist with others in the community of foreigners. There were times, of course, when a confirmed bachelor was a welcome guest at a dinner party. There were times when Bitterwood entertained guests in his own gloomy dining room. Such occasions occurred only after Bitterwood had instructed his servant in cooking. His method was simple: When a meal pleased him, he said, "Rose, that was satisfactory." When a meal displeased him, he said, "Rose, that was not satisfactory."

Bitterwood had gone to China with the intention of becoming a very wealthy man. To this end, he worked hard and successfully at his business. As befits a man who often thought and sometimes said aloud, "Waste not, want not," Mr. Bitterwood exercised tight control over household expenses.

Upon his arrival in China, he had made it his business to learn how much each and every foreign household in that town spent for food and other necessities of life. He then calculated an amount that would correspond to the needs of a bachelor with one small and skinny servant. Convinced as he was that all of the Chinese servants of the foreigners in China were stealing their masters blind, Bitterwood first cut that amount for household expenses in half and gave the money to Rose, instructing her to shop for their needs. Upon seeing how well she succeeded, Bitterwood then cut that amount in half. Poor Rose. Would it have helped her at all if she had known the story of the miller's daughter who was put by the king into a room full of straw and told to spin it into gold? Would she have understood the joy of the greedy king who rewarded the miller's daughter by putting her into a still larger room full of straw?

Bitterwood was frugal. Yes, his life included the necessary sherry and port, but he was frugal. And, yes, his life did include that one luxury. Somewhere in his youth, Mr. Malvern Bitterwood had acquired a taste for coffee. And so it happened, that in the land of tea, brown hemp bags of coffee beans were delivered to him at his place of business. Bitterwood himself taught Rose how to grind the beans, how to brew the coffee. Of this one luxury, Bitterwood allowed himself three cups a day, one each at breakfast, midday, and after supper.

For Rose, there was a week of seven days of work. Bitterwood, who held absolutely no truck with heathenish festivals, never once permitted any celebration of any Chinese holiday by his servant. Once a year, at Christmas, Bitterwood gave to Rose a piece of dark cotton cloth, blue, gray, brown, or black, with which she was to sew herself a new dress. After five or ten Christmases, Bitterwood calculated that she must have accumulated by then a wardrobe that bordered on excessive for her station.

He had been pleased to note on one occasion how she had sewn for herself a padded jacket from pieces of old dresses. Naturally, she had to ask his permission before doing so. Bitterwood knew the ways of thieving servants. No scrap of cloth from his house became a rag without his consent. He himself oversaw all the mending Rose did.

And it was true that Bitterwood's fortune grew during the next five, ten, fifteen, twenty, or was it even thirty years? In that time his mustache, beard, and the hair of his head, went from copper to silver. And while the fortune, which Bitterwood had made secure in the great banks of England and Switzerland, grew, Bitterwood spent little and rejoiced a great deal. When he died, which with his vigorous good health seemed a good many years and an even greater fortune away, that fortune would become the surprise and delight of a great-nephew who had recently been born in faraway England.

In those years—was it twenty or was it thirty?—Mr. Malvern Bitterwood rarely struck Rose, rarely shouted at her. She did her work as she should, quietly and modestly. Did she have a candle in her room? Could she read and write? How did Rose spend her time when Bitterwood was out of the house? When others, dinner guests, praised her, Bitterwood modestly admitted he had been rather successful in training his servant.

It was a night after twenty, or was it thirty, years.

Bitterwood, who had come home rather late, was in his study, sipping a glass of port, finishing a last cigar. Without warning, the front door of the house crashed in, torn from its hinges. Into the study burst four bandits, muddy boots tracking filth through the hall and over the carpets as they came. Seizing hold of Bitterwood, the bandits demanded all his wealth, crying out that they would subject him to the death of a thousand cuts. That punishment Bitterwood knew. It took a good many hours for the victim to die, unless the killer were careless. With a patient executioner, the torment could last for days.

The bandits, all of them armed with great, long swords, encircled him. Bitterwood, convinced they would not be satisfied with what little gold he had in the house, silently prepared to die, when, from the hall outside his study, came a voice. The bandits turned toward the sound. Calling, enticing in Chinese, the voice they heard was seductive, the voice of a young girl, sweet and promising. It came from just beyond the closed door. One, two, three, four, the bandits rushed through the door. The voice ceased.

In the silence that followed, Bitterwood hesitated. Should he rush out into the night, call for help? Cautiously, he moved toward the study door, pushed on it. There was something in the way. Bitterwood pressed his face against the crack, straining to see. Slowly the door opened.

There, on the floor, in four pools of blood, lay the heads

of the four bandits. There on the floor, in a row, lay the bodies of the bandits, one, two, three, four. There, with a sword as tall as herself, stood Rose.

"Rose," said Bitterwood. "You've killed all four of them."

"They have been sent into the other world," replied Rose. "They are my revenge for the bandits who kidnapped me from my family, refused ransom, and to dishonor my family sold me to a foreigner." Carefully stepping around the bodies and the blood, Rose put the sword into the hands of Mr. Malvern Bitterwood. "You have done a brave thing," she said, "to kill these four who are so greatly feared in this province."

"But, I, but you . . ." sputtered Bitterwood.

"For all of us, it is best so," she said firmly.

Was it Bitterwood, then, who was no coward, who suggested that he could never have fought all four, killed all four, without receiving so much as a scratch? Was it Rose, or he himself, who drew out the dagger of one of the four, wiped it on a clean cloth, and cut his arm, drawing blood, so that Bitterwood was a most convincing hero?

One thing is certain. Rose walked out of the hall, wearing a dark dress that was spattered with blood. A few minutes later it was Rose who reappeared from the kitchen, face and hands clean, hair tidy, wearing a clean, worn dark dress with a high collar, long sleeves, a dress slit up either side from the hem, with black trousers underneath. It was Rose who walked out into the dark night, wearing cloth shoes she had sewn with her own two hands. Rose went to tell what had happened.

Later, when he was summoned to an audience with the governor of that province, Bitterwood was rewarded with an exquisite piece of jade on a silken cord. It was whispered that Bitterwood, who had been tutored by Rose, had, during that audience, behaved himself rather well for a foreigner.

After life had returned to its former quiet, Bitterwood called Rose to him in his study. With some pride he drew from a folder a paper, written in English and in Chinese. "This," he said, "is a paper that grants you your freedom."

"Thank you." Rose bowed.

"Will you . . . Do you . . ." Bitterwood stumbled where he had not intended to stumble. "Will you return to your family?"

"No," said Rose. "They have mourned my death."

"If you would agree to stay as my free servant,"— Bitterwood cleared his throat—"then I could offer you a salary of . . ." He named a wage only slightly lower than what the other foreigners payed for a household with a single servant.

"That is acceptable." Rose bowed again.

"And . . ." Here Bitterwood could not keep the joy from creeping into his voice. Bitterwood, thinking of his great-nephew, thinking of this surprise, Bitterwood had become more Chinese than he knew. "And," he repeated, "you and I will go to buy for you a son, a fine, healthy, intelligent boy, whom we will train for a profession so that he can support you in honor when you become old, and can honor your name when you are dead." With a great rush and a sigh, Bitterwood got it all out and was rewarded by the look of surprise and joy on Rose's face—before she became once again the calm woman who bowed and said, "Thank you."

"And Rose," he added in an excess of generosity, "from this day, never ever again must you ask my approval before you take any linens that are worn beyond repair and put them to another purpose. From this day, *you* will decide!"

"Thank you, Mr. Bitterwood," said Rose, bowing yet again. "And from this day"—she stood straight, her eyes, as ever, modestly lowered—"I will no longer urinate into your coffee." ♦

"IS THAT a true story?" asked Jeff, staring hard at the old lady.

"I surely don't know. I've heard it more than once. The first time I heard it, a fine-looking old sailor told me he'd been there, seen it all happen when he was a cabin boy on a sailing ship out of San Francisco. The way he told the story, sailors on the ship had teased and tormented the cook, who had repaid them with *his* special coffee. The cook had been shanghaied to serve on the ship."

"Shanghaied?"

"That's what they called it when people were kidnapped to serve on ships. That's how captains sometimes got enough men to fill out a crew. Sailors and cooks often deserted, too. . . . But I do know a true story, and maybe more than one. You keep on filling those pillows, and sewing up the ends. Only, see here now; some of you need to use stitches that are a bit smaller. You don't mind if stories leak out because they always go in and out of story pillows, but you don't want the rayon fluff to spill out. The pillow would go all flat then."

"Okay." Jeff and several others examined their stitches critically.

"Don't slow down. Just take smaller stitches, and listen." Clearing her throat, she began. "This is an absolutely true bunny story. . . ."

❖ An Absolutely True Bunny Story

B urt was alone in the house, reading his newspaper, when the dog scratched to be let out. Half an hour later Burt was still not finished with the sports section when the dog scratched at the door to be let in again. Without putting down his paper, Burt went to the kitchen door, opened it, and stood aside for the dog to pass. The dog, however, stopped, half in and half out of the door, wagging his tail with great force. Annoyed at the dog's slowness, Burt lowered his newspaper, then dropped it. There in the dog's mouth was the neighbor's pet bunny rabbit, obviously dead.

"Good grief, dog!" Burt bellowed. "What have you done?" Burt was so upset that the dog gave up the bunny without a struggle. Burt put the bunny on the kitchen counter and stared at it, muttering all the while, "No, no-no-no-no-no, no."

What on earth could he do? The neighbor, the neighbor's whole family, would be heartbroken, would never forgive them. How could the dog have done it? And, even more important, what should Burt do now?

Burt could so vividly imagine the pleasant relations

with the neighbor becoming totally unpleasant. What to do?

Then, amazed at his own brilliance, Burt knew exactly how to save the day. Carefully, he washed off the bunny, then ran upstairs, returning in a flash with the hair dryer. Carefully, he dried and fluffed the bunny's fur, looking out the kitchen window every so often to see whether the neighbor's car was in the drive. Once the bunny was thoroughly clean and dry, Burt left the dog in the house and quietly made his way to the bunny's cage in the neighbor's yard.

There. Now the neighbor would find the poor dead bunny all clean and fluffy in his cage as he should be. Then the neighbor would assume the bunny had died a sad, but natural, death. Burt could relax and return to his newspaper.

For the next three days, Burt avoided looking at the bunny cage. Not once during those days did Burt see even a glimpse of his neighbor.

Then, one fine morning about a week later, there was the neighbor, lugging heavy ropes out to the big maple in his yard. Clearly, the neighbor was going to put up his swing, and clearly, putting it up was a job for two.

Burt went outside, said hello, and walked over to help. All the time they worked, Burt kept his eyes averted from the bunny cage. The neighbor, on the contrary, seemed to be looking in that direction all the time. It made Burt a bit edgy, but they got up the swing and stood back to admire it.

It was a fine swing, they both agreed; last year it had been much used by all the kids in the neighborhood.

Once again the neighbor looked to the bunny cage. Burt did not. The neighbor sighed and shook his head. Burt pretended not to notice.

"Strangest thing," said the neighbor. Burt tensed. "Last week, on Friday, our pet bunny got loose," the neighbor began. "Somehow he got out of his cage."

Burt stopped breathing.

The neighbor shook his head. "We can't imagine how. We had no idea. Then, while my wife was backing the car out of the garage, she ran over him. Killed him. We were all broken up, the whole family. We had a bunny funeral and buried him out in the backyard, with flowers and everything. Then, we went to my mother's for the weekend." The neighbor lowered his voice to a whisper. "And when we got back . . . there he was . . . ," the neighbor looked toward the cage, "in his cage . . . all . . . fluffy." ♦

"NOW, MADAM." The voice was huge; but in spite of how hard they looked, no one in the class could see a soul. The old lady smiled with her whole face to hear the owner of the voice, and immediately pulled herself down to sit on a cabinet near the windows.

"You must not tell the next story," the voice insisted. "You need to rest yourself a bit. Your voice is all cracking with the effort. When the kids are working this hard, they need listening that's easy. I'll tell one I've been waiting to tell, the one about Patrick."

❖ Patrick's Cure

P atrick O'Malley was born blighted, though no one ever spoke of it. He was a small boy, well made, handsome, with dark soulful eyes and quite a voice. Oh! his voice was musical, low and sweet. The blight was, however, on poor Patrick. To be born Irish, to hear and to know a good story in the happening and in the telling, to appreciate the stories in your life, and to be unable to tell! What's worse, Patrick couldn't for the life of him stop from trying to tell. Patrick would begin, all eager, but then about two sentences into his telling, he already knew he was failing. He'd get things backward, spoil the timing by going too fast in one place, too slow in another; he'd never stop, not even when he was blushing for shame. No, he'd blunder on, worse and worse until he'd done the story quite in. When Patrick made these attempts, his listeners, trapped, their eyes glazing over, endured. They endured and felt ashamed, for it is a shame to ruin a good story.

As a small boy, Patrick hoped he'd grow out of his affliction, hoped and prayed, and only spoke of it out loud once, to his confessor. The old priest listened carefully and waited a bit before replying.

"Patrick. There are things we learn to do, without noticing we've learned, like walking; and there are things we work at to learn. You could work at learning to tell a story well. Maybe the good Lord intends it as a test and as a lesson to you, and to all of us."

Patrick thanked his confessor and went away. What an idea! The shame of it; taking lessons to learn to tell a story? An Irishman born and bred, to take such lessons? Never!

Instead of studying how to deliver a good story, Patrick decided to go to America, where they'd never notice.

And for a time it seemed he was correct. The Irish in America welcomed the sweet, shy new home-boy, and the non-Irish were charmed by his Irish brogue and gentle manners. For quite a long time these people in America waited patiently when Patrick spoke, waited for him to get to the point.

At last everyone knew, and Patrick knew they knew. It was then that Patrick offered a bargain to God. He, Patrick, would become a priest, and serve God with all his heart and mind and body and soul, and then, he prayed, God would take pity on him and remove the stain. You see, Patrick was convinced in his heart that the dear Lord, if not Irish himself, was more than merely fond of the Irish and would surely answer a prayer so directly linked to Patrick's very Irishness. After all, had not the good Lord made the Irish the finest storytellers in all the world?

"Dear God," Patrick prayed every single day, "it's more

than a pity to be Irish and to ruin a good story. Dear Lord, it's a crime."

Patrick served and Patrick prayed, but wasn't it hard not to lose hope.

As a priest, Patrick was kind and modest, intelligent and faithful. The blight, however, remained. When at mass Patrick spoke, you could be sure that if someone sighed it was not because of emotions stirred, or the mind convinced by his telling. No. If someone sighed, it was because Patrick's speaking was finished.

Now, after many a long year, and many a prayer, a miracle took place. Father Patrick had prayed so hard and served so faithfully that his prayer was answered.

On that certain night, Patrick had fallen asleep, still praying, asking, "Dear Lord, please remove this blight from me, this curse that I, Patrick, Irish to my fingertips, cannot tell a story without spoiling it. Dear Lord, surely you see that an Irishman must be able to tell a story."

When he awoke, it was morning, faintly light and, astonishingly, bitterly cold. He opened his eyes, feeling he was himself and not himself. He rose from his bed, washed and dressed and said his prayers and started out of his room to go to mass. There outside his door was a hallway he'd never before seen, with windows looking out on vast fields of glittering snow. Beyond them was a forest dark with pines. To his left was a staircase. There at the bottom of it stood several priests. They greeted him as if they knew him, but he could swear he'd never laid eyes on them before this minute. Great tall giants they were, with huge, slow motions, and thoughtful expressions on their faces.

Ever courteous, Patrick greeted them. But it was not his speech he uttered; his voice perhaps, but the cadence of his speech was theirs. They were big men, their lives filled more with silence than with talk. They smiled, greeting him. "Good morning, Olaf." When he tried to explain that he was Patrick, Irish, and not of this place, and to ask what was this place, they chuckled affectionately. The tallest of the tall, his beard and hair white as the snow, smiled. "Not of Minnesota, Olaf? You an Irishman, Olaf? And your name is Patrick?"

"Ah, Olaf," said another, shaking his head and continuing to laugh in genuine amusement as they led Patrick, whose prayers had been answered, down the corridor to the church. "Olaf, you are a master. Will you give us another good story after chapel, on our way to breakfast?" ♦

"AWWW," Eustace groaned in sympathy. "Poor Patrick. You guys didn't appreciate my story either."

"Sure we did, Eustace; it would be a great story if you didn't cheat us with that 'and then I woke up' business," Jeff said.

Eustace started to argue, but fell silent when everyone in the class agreed with Jeff.

"Anyway," said Grace and Sidney both, "who told us Patrick's story? Can't we see him?"

"Him?" said the old lady. "He's the frog who lives beside the spring that's under this school. He won't show himself because he says he's too handsome. He claims just one glimpse of him will cause all the girls to want to kiss him. He says that if just one of the girls who kisses him is a princess, then he'll be forced to turn into a prince, and he much prefers being a frog. Personally, I think he has had his head turned by hearing and telling too many old tales."

"Pretty conceited," Tilly agreed.

Jeff, sucking on his bleeding thumb, which he had stuck while sewing shut a purple pillow, struggled to his feet. He was stiff all over, and worried. Once again the clock and his watch had gone into fast forward. Beyond the windows was only darkness. Sidney, as if voicing Jeff's fears, asked, "Why isn't that pretty witch back yet with the others? Do you suppose she couldn't find them down at the spring?"

"Yeah," said Barton. "And we better start carrying these bags of finished pillows out of here. Look how many are done."

Kanjii and Eustace, who had taken a break for a little bit of shadowboxing, stopped in midblow. "Look! The old lady is floating away. Hey! Should we leave now? We're nearly done."

By way of answering, the old lady put her left index finger to her lips. With the other hand, her cane extended, she pointed toward the far wall of the room, that is, to the place where the wall should have been.

All of them looked as she had directed. They could see into what normally was a kindergarten classroom. It was bright as day in there, with fish tank and plants, toys, books and blocks—everything in the usual places. Little children sat in a half circle, facing a woman with lots of curly hair framing her lively, gentle face. By concentrating very hard, Jeff could hear her voice clearly. . . .

❖ Lily

When I was a little girl, I remember that on the first day of kindergarten I wore a blue dress. I remember the dress, and I remember that all day long I thought about the classroom teddy bear. It wasn't that he was brand-new, or especially fancy, but he fit just right in my arms, and when I looked into his brown glass eyes, I could see that he understood everything, that he was my friend.

That night at supper, my mama and papa asked me and my big sister about our day at school. My sister told some things, and I told some things, but I did not mention the classroom teddy bear. Every day at school I pretended the classroom teddy bear was my own, and I tried to keep him by my side. And every night I thought and thought about the teddy bear.

Times were hard. That was what the grown-ups said, and when I was in kindergarten I knew it meant that even people who had jobs, as my papa did—even people with work had very little money to spend.

And so, day after day, I played with the classroom teddy bear, and night after night I thought about the classroom teddy bear. After a few weeks, I told my big sister that the classroom teddy bear was my favorite thing in the whole world. I told her while we were walking home from school. "Just don't think that you'll get a teddy bear," said my practical big sister. "Papa and Mama will work hard and save to get you a doll for your birthday, but you know that Papa says"—and here my big sister made her face and voice into a serious Papa face and Papa voice—" 'teddy bears are an unnecessary frivolity.' " Then my sister asked me how soon I'd be big enough to walk home alone from school. I told her that I was already big enough, and so she walked away to join her big girlfriends.

Weeks later, one afternoon when school let out, I found myself alone in the kindergarten classroom. With no one to see me, I picked up the classroom teddy bear and put him under my coat. I walked out of the school and down the street toward home. But as I walked, I started to think about how my mama would look when she saw me come in the door with the classroom teddy bear. I knew I could not stand to see her look sad, and I *could not* take the teddy bear back to the school. Instead, I took the teddy bear deep into a thicket in the park just in front of our apartment building. I took the bear to a secret place where I used to play. I put him down there and told him to wait for me, that I'd be back to play.

I did go back, and I played with him every minute I was not in school.

At school, everyone looked for the bear. Maybe he had fallen behind the bookcase. Maybe he was under the dress-up clothes. "Has anyone seen the bear?" the kindergarten teacher asked. "No. I haven't seen the bear," said everyone in the class. I said it, too.

Every day I went back to the bear, and every day I loved the bear more.

But the days grew shorter, darker, and colder, and then the rains came, and the wind blew the fallen leaves on the streets and in the thicket. I went every day to play with the bear, even when the cold came, and the snow.

And as often as I went to the thicket and as much as I loved the bear and played with him, the harsh weather wore at him. The day came when his seams opened. The day came when his cloth fell apart in my hands. And, though I have never stopped loving him, the day came when there was no more bear.

I remember kindergarten, and I remember the classroom teddy bear.♦

THE LIGHT in the kindergarten classroom faded; their own room meanwhile grew dark, silent, and very cold. Cabinets, sewing machines, windows, doors, all vanished. Only the story pillows remained, along with the last class of eighth-graders from the Poor Farm Road Elementary School.

In the center of what had been the classroom floor, a stone staircase appeared, faintly lit by something farther along the corridor that led away from the bottom step.

"Look," Kanjii whispered. "It's a way out."

"Yeah," Eustace nodded, "but down."

"Still . . ." Tilly's eyes were bright. "I'll bet the spring is down there. I want to see it."

"But," Eustace gulped, "what if the school building falls on us while we're down there?"

"Look, Eu. It's the only way out," Jeff urged, grabbing the last of the pillows and picking up an already bulging canvas bag.

Silently they packed the pillows into the bags; they made additional carriers by filling their sweatshirts and sweaters with pillows and tying them around their waists. Once all the pillows had been distributed, Kanjii started down the staircase. The path was long and steep, lit from somewhere beyond them, perhaps from the spring itself. They stumbled, hampered by the bags of pillows. For the most part, they went in silence, listening to the shuffling of their own feet on the stone floor. Drawing near to the mouth of an underground cavern, they could smell and hear water.

Jeff and Kanjii were the first to reach the cave. At the opening, they stopped abruptly. Jeff stifled a cry. He felt, for the first time that day, not the excitement of a peculiar adventure, but fear. Ms. Laurel? The others? Were they dead? The only movement, only sounds were those of water running, the stream gushing out of the far wall of the cavern. Jeff and Kanjii stared. The others crowded up behind them, sensed their fear, said nothing, and waited. There they were.

Ms. Holly, who had been the school librarian since

before they were born, was slumped in her wheelchair. Ms. Oakes, who always had time for every child, even the peskiest ones, knelt on the floor, her head resting on her arms, which were folded upon the seat of a stone bench.

One by one the other students squeezed themselves past Jeff and Kanjii, until the whole class stood crowded at the entrance, staring at the four bodies motionless in the cave. The young woman from the mountains sat cross-legged on the floor, her hands in her lap, her long hair covering her face.

And Ms. Laurel? Jeff adored her, her beauty touched with glamour. No woman in town wore shoes with higher heels. Tall, slim, elegant, her black hair pulled back in a smooth chignon, she sat on a stone bench, her back against the wall of the cave. Like the others, her eyes were closed. In profile, Ms. Laurel's smooth, dark face was more beautiful than Nefertiti, had purer lines than any Greek statue. If she would wake up and look at them, Jeff just knew her face would have the look it always held for them, one of patient intelligence that calmly believed in you, a sense of humor that helped you put things just about where they ought to be put. If only she would wake up! Jeff's heart thundered in his chest. But what if the spring had taken the three women who had linked it to the school? Had the spring taken the girl who came from the mountains? You heard about things like that, magic demanding payment. Jeff choked. He could not say the question out loud. Are we supposed to put this scene in our memories, find words for it? How about us? Is the spring going to keep us? Keep all memories, all stories, everything?

The spring, all the while, flowed steadily from a crack in the wall of the cave, falling in a silver stream down to a rock basin just above the floor of the cave. From the basin it ran again underground, out of sight. The falling water threw out droplets that sparkled on the faces of those standing close to it.

After a time, Tilly whispered, her voice nevertheless echoing in the cavern. "In cases of enchantment, you might have to kiss the sleeping, or sprinkle water from the spring on them. Then they'll wake up." Sidney, who was of a far more practical nature, snorted. "People who are asleep usually wake up if you touch them lightly," which she then did.

Indeed, the sleepers awoke, and appeared surprised to see the whole class staring at them. Jeff, feeling both relief that the women were alive, and shame that he had assumed the worst, blushed. Nobody noticed because everyone else was asking and answering questions. Ms. Oakes had been led to the spring while searching for the bags and bags of fabric she *knew* she had put away for the pillows. Each of the others, in the course of looking for the missing ones, had come to this spot and remained. Ms. Laurel supposed that the four grown-ups had not been necessary to the task at hand and so had been sent to take a nap. Even Jeff laughed.

"We had our nap, too, up in the classroom; seems like years ago," Tilly said.

"If we are at a spring, especially a magic one . . . ," Jeff, recovered from his dread and from his shame, began.

"Oh yeah!" Sidney cut in. "We might never see it again. We should drink."

They looked at Ms. Laurel, who nodded her agreement. "Then," said Ms. Oakes, "we should leave. I have the feeling that it is time." The young woman from the mountains whispered her concurrence.

One by one they drank.

Ms. Laurel led the way through the corridor down which they had come, and then off through a different corridor, one they had not seen before, one that took a series of bewildering turns. Jeff, Sidney, and Tilly helped with the wheelchair, which Ms. Holly had insisted must go last.

They passed places that echoed in the darkness, passed places that smelled of cows and horses and, in one spot, something else. Li An, who lived on a farm and knew, said, "Pigs." As they went, they heard the earth behind them rumble in the darkness, felt a shaking beneath their feet.

All at once, the ones in front warned, "Steep upgrade! Slippery!" Jeff smelled fresh air, heard the kids in front groan, then shout, "Shade your eyes!"

Jeff squinted, pushed, lifted, up and out, the chair taking several rough bumps. The ones in front were right about the sunlight. It was painfully bright. All that time inside they'd been misled, fooled by clocks and by the darkness that had appeared outside the classroom windows.

Here, where they were truly outside the school building, the midday sun was brilliant. Jeff thought he'd stop and catch his breath, but one step out of the tunnel and he felt a jolt that nearly knocked him down.

Behind them, beneath them, the earth shuddered. Sidney took one side of the wheelchair, Jeff the other. They ran, following the others. Tilly fell over bags of pillows, stood up, hurled the bags ahead of her. Others raced back to help with the wheelchair, and to help Tilly. Everyone ran.

Panting, tumbling, falling, the members of the last eighth-grade class of the Poor Farm Road Elementary School reached the row of fir trees at the edge of the parking lot.

They thrust those hundreds of pillows into Ms. Holly's van, each keeping only one, and retrieved their sweatshirts, which were no longer needed to transport pillows. They turned to look back toward the building from where they had come.♦

ON A COLD, brilliant Saturday in November, in a middle-sized town in the middle of nowhere, a middle-sized school building that had stood for more than one hundred years collapsed. It went down with a whoosh, sucked into the earth, swallowed up so that not a trace of it showed.

Within half an hour, the whole town turned out to see what there was to see, and to speculate. Small children, their breath white puffs in the sunshine, darted in and out among the crowd. The students of that last eighth-grade class moved in and out of groups, now with their families, now with their friends. Nothing was remarkable in the crowd, only in the spectacular collapse of the school. Grown-ups stood in clusters to watch and talk. Had there been caves under there, maybe old mines nobody knew about? Within minutes, the school building was gone, sunk into some depths no one was quite prepared to measure. The ground where it had stood heaved and thrust enormous boulders to the surface in the middle of the crater. Water came up and around the boulders to fill the hole.

"That water," somebody announced, "comes from a spring the old timers used to talk about."

"Oh yes," someone else agreed. "They said the water was sweet and cold and flowed very fast."

Talk of the spring reminded someone of a story he knew, about a quarry. People had been taking rock from that quarry for years. Sure, there had been a little water, nothing to speak of. And then one morning the workers arrived to find the quarry full, nearly to the top of the cliffs, full of water. In one night it went from quarry to swimming hole, and a good sized one at that. Pretty place it was, and "just look at how pretty this one is already. Just look at the water flowing over those boulders and down into the crater. Clear as light, that water, not a trace of building debris, not dust, not mud. Clear as light."

After that day in November, nothing remained of the Poor Farm Road Elementary School except the stories people knew, and the ones they made up.

AUTHOR'S NOTE

Of the stories, those about the thorn branch, the gasoline pump, and the classroom teddy bear are based on stories told to me by the people to whom they happened. The story of revenge is my version of a very old story that was first told to me by a man who was born in 1864, who said he was cabin boy on a sailing ship when a cook took such revenge on sailors who had mistreated him. Later, in a book by Pearl Buck, I read of a servant who repaid a cruel master in that way. I took my own small daughters, at their request, to see the special Halloween scenes described in "Remember?" The story of Juno is based on something one of my children heard on the radio and believed at the time was a true news story. I wrote "Juno," and then learned this year that the story of a dog who bites off the finger of a burglar, who is then found hiding in a closet, is what students of our culture call "an urban myth"—that is, a story we all hear as "true" but which is simply another scary story. The bunny story is another of those stories we are told happened to a friend of a friend. The rest of the stories are ones I have imagined.